THE WRECK OF THE "

AN ACCOUNT OF
THE MUTINY OF THE CREW
AND THE
LOSS OF THE SHIP
WHEN TRYING TO MAKE THE
BERMUDAS.

VOL. II.

BY WILLIAM CLARK RUSSELL

CHAPTER I.

As the men had been up all night, I recommended the carpenter to go to them and tell them that the watches would not be altered, and that the watch whose spell it was below should turn in.

Some, it appeared, asked that rum should be served out to them; but the carpenter answered that none should be given them until breakfast time, and that if they got talking too much about the drink, he'd run a bradawl into the casks and let the contents drain out; for if the men fell to[2] drinking, the ship was sure to get into a mess, in which case they might be boarded by the crew of another vessel and carried to England, where nothing less than hanging or transportation awaited them.

This substantial advice from the lips of the man who had been foremost in planning the mutiny produced a good effect, and the fellows who had asked for spirits were at once clamorously assailed by their mates; so that, in their temper, had the carpenter proposed to fling the rum casks overboard, most of the hands would have consented and the thing being done.

All this I was told by the boatswain, who had left the poop with the carpenter, but returned before him. I took this opportunity of being alone with the man to ask him some questions relative to the mutiny, and particularly inquired if he could tell me what was that intention which the man[3] named "Bill" had asked the carpenter to communicate to me, but which he had refused to explain. The boatswain, who was at bottom a very honest man, declared that he had no notion of the intention the carpenter was concealing, but promised to try and worm the secret out of Johnson or others who were in it, and impart it to me.

He now informed me that he had come into the mutiny because he saw the men were resolved, and also because they thought he took the captain's part, which was a belief full of peril to him. He said that he could not foresee how this trouble would end; for though the idea of the men to quit the ship and make for the shore in open boats was feasible, yet they would run very heavy risks of capture any way; for if they came across a ship while in the boats they could not refuse to allow themselves to be taken on board, where, some of the mutineers[4] being very gross and ignorant men, the truth would certainly leak out; whilst as to escaping on shore, it was fifty to one if the answers they made to inquiries would not differ so widely one from another as to betray them.

But at this point our conversation was interrupted by the carpenter coming aft to ask me to keep watch whilst he and the boatswain turned in, as he for one was "dead beat," and would not be of any service until he had rested.

It was now broad daylight, the east filled with the silver splendours of the rising sun. I descried a sail to windward, on the starboard tack, heading eastward. I made her out through the glass to be a small topsail schooner, but as we were going free with a fresh breeze we soon sank her hull.

The sight of this vessel, however, set me thinking on my own position. What would[5] be thought and how should I be dealt with when (supposing I should ever reach land) I should come to tell the story of this mutiny? But this was a secondary consideration. My real anxiety was to foresee how the men would act when I had brought them to the place they wished to arrive at. Would they give such a witness against their murderous dealings as I was, a chance to save my life?—I, whose plain testimony could set justice on the hunt for every one of them. I could not place confidence in their assurances. The oaths of such ruffians as many of them undoubtedly were, were worthless. They would murder me without an instant's scruple if by so doing they could improve their own chances of escape; and I was fully persuaded that I should have shared the fate of Coxon and Duckling in spite of the sympathy I had shown them, and their declaration that they did not want6 my life, had they not foreseen that they would stand in need of some competent person to navigate the ship for them, and that I was more likely to come into their projects than either of the men they had murdered.

My agitation was greater than I like to admit; and I turned over in my mind all sorts of ideas for my escape, but never forgetting the two helpless persons whose lives I considered wholly dependent on my own preservation.

At one moment I thought of taking the boatswain into my confidence, stealthily storing provisions in one of the quarter-boats, and watching an opportunity to sneak off with him and our passengers under cover of night.

Then I thought of getting him to sound the minds of the crew, to judge if there were any who might assist us should we7 rise upon the more desperate of the mutineers.

Another notion was to pretend to mistake the ship's whereabouts, and run her into some port.

But such stratagems as these, easily invented, were in reality impracticable.

To let the men see that I stood to my work, I never quitted the deck until six o'clock. The morning was then very beautiful, with a rich and warm aroma in the glorious southerly breeze, and the water as blue as the heavens.

On arousing the carpenter in the cabin formerly occupied by me (I found him in the bunk on my mattress with his boots on, and a pipe belonging to me in his hand), I told him that the ship could now carry all plain sail, and advised him to make it. He got out of the bunk in a pretty good temper, and went along the cuddy; but as he was8 about to mount the companion-ladder I called to know if he would see the steward, and speak to him about serving out the cuddy stores, as I preferred that he should give the man instructions, since they would best represent the wishes of the crew. But the truth was, I wanted to pack all the responsibility that I could upon him, so as to make myself as little answerable as possible to the men.

"Yes, yes. Fetch him out. Where is he?" he replied, turning round.

"Steward!" I called.

After a pause the door of the captain's cabin opened, and the figure of the steward stepped forth. Such a woebegone object, with bloodless face and haggard expression, and red eyes and quivering mouth, hands hanging like an idiot's, his hair matted, his knees knocking together as he walked, I never wish to see again.

9 "Now, young feller," said the carpenter (the steward, by the way, was about forty years old), "what do you think ought to be done to you, hey? Is hangin' too mild, or is drownin' more to your fancy? or would you like to be di-sected by the cook, who is reckoned a neat hand at carvin'?"

The steward turned his bloodshot eyes upon me, and his white lips moved.

"Mr. Stevens is only joking," I exclaimed, feeling that I would give a year's pay to strike the ruffian to the earth for his brutal playing with the miserable creature's terror. "He wants to talk to you about the cuddy provisions."

The carpenter stared at him grimly, out of a mean tyranny and relish of his fears; and the poor creature said, "Yes, sir?" lifting his eyes humbly to the carpenter's face, and folding his hands in an involuntary attitude of supplication.

10 "You'll understand, young feller," said the carpenter, thrusting his hands into his pockets and leaning against the mizzen-mast, "that we're all equals aboard this here wessel now. No one's above t'other, barring yourself, who's just nowheeres at all, owin' to your keeping in tow of the skipper when he was pisoning us with the stores which you, d——yer! took joy in sarving out! Now, you understand this: you're to turn to and sarve out the

cuddy stores to the men at the proper time, and three tots o' grog every day to each man. Mr. Ryle 'll tell you how long our passage 'll last, and you're to make a calkilation of the live stock so as each watch gits a share of the pigs an' poultry. But you," he continued, squirting some tobacco juice from his mouth, "aren't to touch no other provisions but the stores which the crew's been eatin' of: mind that! If we catch you tastin' so11 much as half a cuddy biscuit, by the living thunder! we'll run you up to the fore-yard-arm!"

He shook his fist in the steward's face, and addressing me, said—

"That's all to be said, ain't it?"

"That's all," I replied; and the steward went cringing and reeling towards the pantry, whilst the carpenter mounted the companion-ladder.

I entered the cabin, which, to save confusion, I will continue to call the captain's cabin, and seated myself in a chair screwed down to the deck before a wide table. This cabin was comfortably furnished with hanging bookshelves, a fine map of the world, a few coloured prints of ships, a handsome cot, and mahogany lockers cushioned on top to serve for seats.

Among some writing materials, a case of mathematical instruments, a boat's compass,12 and a variety of other matters which covered the table, I observed an American five-chambered revolver, which, on examining, I found was loaded. I at once put this weapon in my pocket, and after searching awhile, discovered a box of cartridges, which I also pocketed.

This I considered a very lucky find, as I never knew the moment when I might stand in need of such a weapon; and whether I should have occasion to use it or not, it was certainly better in my possession than in the hands of the men.

I now left my chair to examine the lockers, in the hopes of finding other firearms; and I cannot express the eagerness with which I prosecuted the search, because I considered that, should the boatswain succeed in winning even one man over from the crew, three resolute men, each armed with a revolver or firearm of any kind,13 might, by carefully waiting their opportunity, kill or wound enough of the crew to render the others an easy conquest.

However, to my unspeakable disappointment, my search proved fruitless; all that I found in the lockers were clothes belonging to Captain Coxon, a quantity of papers, old charts, and log-books, some parcels of cigars, and a bag containing about £30 in silver.

Whilst engaged in these explorations, a knock fell on the door, and on my replying, the girl came in. I bowed and asked her to be seated, and inquired how her father did.

"He is still very weak," she answered; "but he is not worse this morning. I heard your voice just now, and watched you enter this cabin. I hope you will let me speak to you. I have so much to say."

"Indeed," I replied, "I have been waiting14 impatiently for this opportunity. Will you first tell me your name?"

"Mary Robertson. My father is a Liverpool merchant, Mr. Royle, and the ship in which we were wrecked was his own vessel. Oh!" she exclaimed, pressing her hands to her face, "we were many hours expecting every moment to die. I cannot believe that we are saved! and sometimes I cannot believe that what has happened is real! I think I was going mad when I saw your ship. I thought the boat was a phantom, and that it would vanish suddenly. It was horrible to be imprisoned with the dead body and that mad sailor! The sailor went mad on the first day, and soon afterwards the passenger—for he was a passenger who lay dead on the deck—sat up in his bed and uttered a dreadful cry, and fell forward dead. The mad sailor pointed to him and howled! and neither papa nor I could get15 out of the house, for the water washed against it and would have swept us overboard."

She told me all this with her hands to her face, and her fair hair flowing over her shoulders, and made a sweet and pathetic picture in this attitude.

Suddenly she looked up with a smile of wonderful sweetness, and, seizing my hand, cried—

"What do we not owe you for your noble efforts? How good and brave you are!"

"You praise me too warmly, Miss Robertson. God knows there was nothing noble in my efforts, nor any daring in them. Had I really risked my life to save you, I should still have barely done my duty. How were you treated yesterday? Well, I hope."

"Oh yes. The captain told the steward to give us what we wanted. I think the16 wine he sent us saved papa's life. He was sinking, but rallied after he had drunk a little of it. I am in a sad plight," she exclaimed, while a faint tinge of red came into her cheeks. "I have not even a piece of ribband to tie up my hair with."

She took her beautiful hair in her hands, and smiled.

"Is there nothing in this cabin that will be of use to you?" I said. "Here is a hair-brush—and it looks a pretty good one. I don't know whether we shall be able to muster a bit of ribband among us, but I just now came across a roll of serge, and if you can do anything with that and a needle and thread, which I'll easily get for you, I'll see that they are put in your cabin. Here are enough clothes to rig out your father, at all events, until his own are made ship-shape. But how am I to help you? That has been on my mind."

17 "I can use the serge if I may have it," she replied, in the prettiest way imaginable.

"Here it is," I said, hauling it out of the locker; "and I'll get needles and thread for you presently. No sailor goes to sea without a housewife, and you shall have mine. And if you will wait a moment I think I can find something else that may be useful."

Saying which I hurried to my old cabin, unlocked my chest, and took out a new pair of carpet slippers.

"A piece of bunting or serge fitted into these will make them sit on your feet," I exclaimed, handing them to her. "And I have other ideas, Miss Robertson, all which I hope will help to make you a little more comfortable by-and-by. Leave a sailor alone to find out ways and means."

She took the slippers with a graceful little smile, and put them alongside the roll18 of serge; and then, with a grave face, and in an earnest voice, she asked me to tell her what the men meant to do with the ship now that they had seized her.

I freely told her as much as I knew, but expressed no fears as to my own, and hers, and her father's safety. Indeed, I took the most cheerful view I could of our situation.

"My notion," said I, "is that when the time comes for the men to leave the ship they will not allow us to go with them. They will oblige us to remain in her, which is the best thing that could happen; for I am sure that the boatswain will stay, and with his and the steward's help there is nothing to prevent us taking the ship into the nearest port, or lying to until we sight a vessel, and then signalling for help."

I fancy she was about to express her doubts of this result, but exclaimed instead—

"No matter what comes, Mr. Royle, we19 shall feel safe with you." And then, suddenly rising, she asked me to come and see her father.

I followed her at once into the cabin.

The old man lay in an upper bunk, with a blanket over him. He looked like a dead man, with his white face rendered yet more death-like in appearance by the dishevelled white hair upon his head, and the long white beard. He was lying perfectly still, with his eyes closed, his thin hands folded outside the blanket.

"Ay, poor Jameson—poor, poor fellow!"

He hid his face, and was silent, I should say, a whole minute, neither Miss Robertson nor myself speaking. Presently, looking up, he continued—

"It came on to blow very heavily, most suddenly, a dreadful gale. It caught the ship in a calm, and she was unprepared, and it snapped all three masts away. Oh, God, what a night of horror! The men went mad, and cried that the ship was going stern down, and crowded into the boats. One went whirling away into the darkness, and one was capsized; and then the captain said the ship was sinking, and my daughter and I ran out of the cabin on to the deck. Well, sir," continued the old man, swallowing25 convulsive sobs as he spoke, "the ship's side had been pierced, the captain said, by one of the yards; and she was slowly settling, and the water came over the deck, and we got into the house where you found us, for shelter. I put my head to the window and called the captain to come, and as he was coming the water hurled him overboard; and there were only myself and my poor girl and Mr. Jameson and—and—tell him the rest!" he suddenly cried, hiding his eyes and stretching out his hand.

"Another time, Miss Robertson," I exclaimed, seeing the look of horror that had come into her face during her father's recital of the story. "Tell me where you live in England, and let us fancy ourselves in the dear old country, which, so it please God, we shall all reach safely in a little time."

But they were both too overcome to26 answer me. The old man kept his face concealed, and the girl drew long sobbing breaths with dry eyes.

However, she plucked up presently, and answered that they lived just out of Liverpool, but that her father had also an estate at Leamington, near Warwick, where her mother died, and where she spent most of her time, as she did not like Liverpool.

"Tell me, sir," cried Mr. Robertson, "did you bring the body of poor Jameson with you? I forget."

"If that was Mr. Jameson whose body lay in the deck-house," I replied, "I left him on the wreck. There was his coffin, Mr. Robertson, and I dared not wait to bring off a dead man when living creatures stood in peril of their lives."

"To be sure, sir!" exclaimed the old gentleman. "You were very right. You acted with great nobleness, and are most27 kind to us now—most kind, Mary, is he not? Let me see?" knitting his brows. "You are not captain of this ship? I think, my dear, you said that this gentleman was the mate? Who is the captain, sir?"

His daughter put her finger to her mouth, which puzzled me until I considered that she either did not want him to know that the captain was murdered, or, supposing he knew of the murder, that the circumstance should not be revived in his memory, which was just now very feeble.

He did not wait for his question to be answered, but asked me where the ship was bound to?

"New Orleans," I answered, with a glance at his daughter.

"New Orleans!" he exclaimed. "Let me think—that is beyond the West Indies." And with great eagerness he said, "Will28 you put into one of the West India Islands? I am known at Kingston; I have shipped largely to a firm there, Messieurs Raymondi and Company. Why, my dear, we shall be very well received, and we shall be able to purchase fresh clothes," he continued, holding up his arm and looking at it with a melancholy smile, "and go home in one of the fine mail packets. Ha! ha! ha! how things come about!"

He lay back upon his pillow with this short mirthless laugh, and remained silent. I do not say that his mind was unhinged, but his intellect was unquestionably impaired by the horrors he had witnessed and the sufferings he had endured. But then he was an old

I thought he slept, and motioned to his daughter; but she stooped and whispered "Papa, here is Mr. Royle;" whereupon he opened his eyes and looked at me. The sense of my presence appeared to be very slowly conveyed to his mind, and then he extended his hand. I took it, and saw with emotion that tears streamed from his eyes.

20 "Sir," he exclaimed, in a weak faltering voice, "I can only say, God bless you!"

I answered cheerfully, "Pray say no more, Mr. Robertson. I want to see you recover your strength. Thank God, your daughter has survived her horrible trials, and will soon quite recover from the effects of them. What now can I do for you? Have you slept?"

"Yes, yes, I have slept; a little, I thank you. Sir, I have witnessed shocking scenes."

I whispered to Miss Robertson—

"Let me prescribe some medicine that will do you both good. What you both require is support. I will be with you in a minute."

So saying, I quitted the cabin and entered the pantry. There I found the steward sitting on the plate chest, with his hands to his temples.

21 "Now then, my lad," said I; "rouse up. You are not dead yet. Have you any brandy here?"

He pointed in a mechanical way to a shelf, where were several bottles. I found what I wanted, and gave him a dose to put heart into him, and asked him for some eggs. Four or five, the gathering of yesterday from the kindly hens under the long-boat, lay in the drawer, which he pulled open. I proceeded to mix two tumblers of eggs and brandy, which I carried to the next cabin.

"This is my physic, Miss Robertson," I exclaimed, putting one of the tumblers into her hand; "oblige me by drinking it; and you, sir," I continued, addressing the old gentleman, "will not wait for her example."

They both, to my great satisfaction, swallowed the contents of the glasses, the 22 effect of which, after some moments, upon Mr. Robertson was decidedly beneficial, for he thanked me for my kindness in a much stronger voice, and even made shift to prop himself up on his elbow.

"It is the best tonic in the world," said I, taking Miss Robertson's glass, "and I am very much obliged to you for your obedience."

The look she gave me was more eloquent than any verbal reply; at least, I found it so. Her face was so womanly and beautiful, so full of pathos in its pallor, with something so brave and open in its whole expression, that it was delightful to me to watch it.

"Now," said I to the old gentleman, "allow me to leave you for a little. I want to see what the Grosvenor can furnish in the shape of linen and drapery. Isn't that what they call it ashore? We have found some 23 serge, and needles and thread are easily got; and I'll set what wits the unfortunate steward has left in him to work to discover how Miss Robertson may be made comfortable until we put you both ashore."

"Do not leave us!" cried the old man. "Your society does me good, sir. It puts life into me. I want to tell you who we are, and about our shipwreck, and where we were going. The Cecilia was my own vessel. I am a merchant, doing most of my trade with the Cape—the Cape of Good Hope. I took my daughter—my only child, sir—to Cape Town, last year, for a change of scene and air; and I should have stopped another year, but Mary got tired and wanted to get home, and—and—well, as I was telling you, Mr—Mr.———"

"Royle," said Miss Robertson.

"Mr. Royle, as I was telling you, Mary got tired; and as the Cecilia was loading at 24 Cape Town—she was a snug sound ship—yes, indeed; and we went on board, we and a gentleman named—named———"

"Jameson," his daughter suggested.

5

man—nearer seventy than sixty, I took him to be; whilst his daughter, whom a little rest had put upon the high road to recovery, did not appear to be above twenty years old.

29 As the time was passing rapidly, I determined to seize the opportunity of the carpenter being on deck to do what I could to make these sufferers comfortable. I therefore left them and sang out to the steward, who came with terrified promptitude, casting the while and almost at every step, fearful glances in the direction of the main-deck, where some of the hands were visible.

I gave him the captain's hair-brush to wash, and covered a tray with the various toilet conveniences with which the ill-fated skipper had provided himself. These I dispatched by the steward to Miss Robertson, and I then made the man prepare a tray with a substantial breakfast, consisting of cold fowl, fine white biscuit, ham, preserved fruit, and some tea, which I boiled in the pantry by means of a spirit-lamp that belonged to me.

30 I took an immense pleasure in supplying these new friends' wants, and almost forgot the perilous situation I was in, in the agreeable labour of devising means to comfort the girl, whose life and her father's, thanks to God, I had been instrumental in preserving.

I made a thorough overhaul of Coxon's effects, holding myself fully privileged to use them for the benefit of poor Mr. Robertson, and sent to his cabin a good suit of clothes, some clean linen, and a warm overcoat.

The steward obeyed me humbly and officiously. He considered his life still in great danger, and that he must fall a sacrifice to the fury of the crew if he quitted the cuddy. However, I found him very useful, for he furnished me with some very good hints, and, among other things, he, to my great delight, informed me that he had 31 in the steerage a box of woman's underclothing, which had been made by his wife's hand for a sister living in Valparaiso, to whom he was taking out the box as a gift, and that I was very welcome to the contents.

I requested him at once to descend with me and get the box out; but this job took us over twenty minutes, for the box was right aft, and we had to clear away upwards of five hundred bird-cages, and a mass of light wooden packages of toys and dolls to come at it. We succeeded at last in hauling it into the cuddy, and he fetched the key and raised the lid; but burst into tears when he saw a letter from his wife, addressed to his sister, lying on top of the linen.

I told him to put the letter in his pocket, and to be sure that his sister would be liberally compensated, if all went well 32 with us, for this appropriation of her property.

"I am not thinking of the clothes, sir," whined the poor fellow, "but of my wife and child, who I may never see again."

"Nonsense," I exclaimed; "try to understand that a man is never dead until the breath is out of his body. You are as well off as I am, and those poor people in the cabin there. What we have to do now is to help each other, and put a bold face on our troubles. The worst hasn't arrived yet, and it won't do to go mad with anticipating it. Wait till it comes, and if there's a road out of it, I'll take it, trust me. Cock this box under your arm, and take it to Miss Robertson."

I had now done everything that was possible, and to my perfect satisfaction; for besides having furnished the old gentleman 33 with a complete change of clothes, I had supplied his daughter with what I knew she would appreciate as a great luxury—a quantity of warm, dry underclothing.

It may strike the reader as ludicrous to find me descending into such trivialities, and perhaps I smiled myself when I thought over the business that had kept me employed since six o'clock. But shipwreck is a terrible leveller, and cold and hunger and misery know but little dignity. How would it seem to Miss Robertson, the daughter of a man obviously opulent, to find herself destitute of clothing, and accepting with gratitude such rude articles of dress as one poor workwoman would make for another of her condition? She, with the memory in her of abundant wardrobes, of costly silks, and furs, and jewellery, of rich attire, and the plentiful apparel of an heiress! But the sea pays but little attention to such claims, and would as lief strip a monarch as a poor sailor, and set him afloat naked to struggle awhile and drown.

CHAPTER II.

At seven bells, that is, half an hour before eight, I heard the carpenter's voice shouting down the companion for the steward. I instantly opened the cabin door to tell the man to go at once, as I believed that Stevens merely called to give him orders about the men's breakfast.

This proved to be the case, as I presently learnt on going on deck, whither I repaired (although it was my watch below) in order to see what the carpenter was about.

I found him lying upon one of the skylights, with a signal-flag under his head, smoking a pipe, whilst three or four of the men sat round him smoking also. All plain sail had been made, as I had directed, and the ship heading west-south-west under a glorious sky, and all around a brilliantly clear horizon and an azure sea.

Away on our lee quarter was a large steamer steering south, brig-rigged, bound, I took it, to the west coast of Africa. The men about the carpenter made a movement when they saw me, as though they would leave the poop, but one of them made some remark in a low voice, which kept them all still. The carpenter, seeing me watching the steamer, called out—

"She wouldn't take long to catch us, would she? I hope there's no man on board this vessel as 'ud like to see her alongside, or would do anything to bring her near. I wouldn't like to be the man as 'ud do it—would you, Joe?"

"Well, I'd rather ha' made my vill fust than forgot it, if so it were that I was that man," responded the fellow questioned.

"We're glad you've come up," continued the carpenter, addressing me, though without shifting his posture, "for blowed if I know what to do if she should get askin' us any questions. What 'll you do, Mr. Royle?"

"Let her signal us first," I replied, quite alive to the sinister suggestiveness of these questions.

"Put the helm up and go astern of her—that's what my advice is," said one of the men.

"You'll provoke suspicion if you do that," I exclaimed. "However, you can act as you please."

"Mr. Royle's quite right," said the man addressed as Joe. "Why can't you leave him alone? He knows more about it than us, mates."

"She's going twelve knots," I said, "and will cross our bows soon enough. Let her signal, we're not bound to answer."

The men, in spite of themselves, watched her anxiously, and so did others on the forecastle, such cowards does conscience make of men. As for myself, I gazed at her with bitter indifference. The help that I stood in need of was not likely to come from such as she, or indeed from any vessel short of an inquisitive Government ship. Moreover, the part I was playing was too difficult to permit me to allow any impulse to inspire. The smallest distrust that I should occasion might cost me my life. My rôle then surely was to seem one with the men, heart and soul.

"Let her go off a point," I exclaimed to the man steering. "They'll not notice that, and she'll be across us the sooner for it."

We were slipping through the water quickly, and by the time she was on our 39 weather bow the steamer was near enough to enable us to see the awning stretched over her after-deck, and a crowd of persons watching us. She was a great ocean steamer, and went magnificently through the water. In a few minutes she was dead on end, dwindling the people watching us, but leaving such a long wake astern of her that we went over it.

What would I have given to be on board of her!

"Let her come to again!" I sang out.

The carpenter now got off the skylight.

"I've told the steward to turn to and get the men's breakfast," said he. "Ourn's to be ready by eight; and I reckon I'll show that snivelling cockney what it is to be hungry. You don't call this a mutiny, do yer, Mr. Royle? Why, the men are like lambs."

"Yes, so they are," I answered. "All 40 the same, I shall be glad to feel dry land under me. The law always hangs the skipper of a mutiny, you know; and I'm skipper by your appointment. So the sooner we all get out of this mess the better, eh, Mr. Stevens?"

"That's right enough," said he; "and we look to you to get us out of it."

"I'll do what you ask me—I won't do more," I answered.

"We don't want more. Enough's what we want. You'll let us see your reckonings every day—not because we doubt you—but it'll ease the minds of the men to know that we aren't like to foul the Bermudas."

"The Bermudas are well to the nor'rard of our course," I answered promptly.

"All right, Mr. Royle, we look to you," he said, with a face on him and in a tone that meant a good deal more than met the ear. "Now, mates," addressing the others, 41 "cut for'ard and get your breakfasts, my lads. It's eight bells. Mr. Royle, I'll go below and call the boatswain; and shall him and me have our breakfast and you arterwards, or you fust? Say the word. I'm agreeable vichever way it goes."

"I'll stop on deck till you've done," I replied, wishing to have the table to myself.

Down he went, and I advanced to the poop-rail and leaned over it to watch the men come aft to receive their share of the cuddy stores.

I will do them the justice to say they were quiet enough. Whether the perception that they no longer recognized any superiors would not presently prevail; whether quarrels, deeds of violence, and all the consequences which generally attend the rebellion of ignorant men would not follow, was another matter. They were decent enough in their behaviour now; 42 congregating on the main-deck and entering the cuddy one by one to receive the stores which the steward was serving out.

These stores, so far as I could judge by the contents of the tin dishes which the men took forward, consisted of butter, white biscuit, a rasher of ham to each man, and tea or cocoa; excellent fare for men who had been starved on rotten provisions. I also found that every man had been served with a glass of rum. They did not seem to begrudge the privilege assumed by the carpenter and boatswain of occupying the cuddy and eating at the table there. The impression conveyed to me on the whole by their aspect and demeanour was that of men subdued and to a certain extent alarmed by the position in which they had placed themselves. But for the carpenter, I believe that I at that time and working upon their then state of mind, could have won them 43 over to submission and made them willing to bring the ship into port and face an inquiry into the circumstances of the revolt. But though I believe this now, I conceived the attempt too full of peril to undertake, seeing that my failure must not only jeopardize my own, but the lives of poor old Mr. Robertson and his daughter, in the safety of whom I was so concerned, that I do not say that my profound anxiety did not paralyse the energy with which I should have attempted my own rescue had I been alone.

How the men treated the steward I could not tell; but I noticed that Master Cook was very quiet in his manner. This was a sure sign of the efficacy of the fright he had received, and it pleased me greatly, as I had feared he would prove a dangerous and bloodthirsty mutineer and a terrible influence in the councils of the men.

44 The carpenter was the first to come on deck. I had seen him (through the skylight) eating like a cormorant, his arms squared, his brown tattooed hand busy with his mouth, making atonement for his long fast in the forecastle. He kept his cap on, but the boatswain had better manners, and looked, as he faced his mate, a quite superior and different order of man altogether.

I went below as soon as Stevens appeared, and the boatswain had the grace to rise, as though he would leave the table, when he saw me. I begged him to keep his seat, and, calling to the steward, asked to know how the men had treated him.

"Pretty middling, sir, thank you, sir," he replied, with a trifle more spirit in his manner. "They're not brutal, sir. The cook never spoke, sir. Mr. Stevens is rather unkind, but I daresay it's only a way he has."

45 The boatswain laughed, and asked him if he had breakfasted.

"No, sir—not yet. I can wait, sir."

"There's plenty to eat and drink," said the boatswain, pointing to the table.

"Yes, sir, plenty," responded the steward, who, looking on the boatswain as one of the ringleaders, was as much afraid of him as of the carpenter.

"Well, then," continued the boatswain, "why don't you tuck in? Mr. Royle won't mind. Sit there, or take what you want into the pantry."

The steward turned pale, remembering the threats that had been used towards him if he touched the cuddy stores, and looked upon the boatswain's civility as a trick to get him hanged.

"Thank you, sir," he stammered; "I've no happetite. I'd rather not eat anything at present, sir. I'll take a ship's biscuit shortly, sir, with your leave."

46 Saying which, and with a ghastly face, he shuffled into the pantry, no doubt to escape from what he would consider highly murderous attentions.

"Rum customer, that steward, Mr. Royle," said the boatswain, rubbing his mouth on the back of his hand.

"So should I be had I undergone his sensations," I replied.

"Well, I don't know about that. You see there ain't nothing regular about a steward. He isn't a sailor and he isn't a landsman; and when you come to them kind o' mongrels, you can't expect much sperrit. It isn't fair to expect it. It's like fallin' foul of a marmozeet, because he isn't as big as a monkey. What about them passengers o' yours, sir? They've not been sarved with breakfast since I've been here?"

"I have seen to them," I answered.47 "What has Stevens been talking about?" As I said this I cast my eyes on the open skylight to see that our friend was not within hearing.

He shook his head, and after a short pause exclaimed—

"He's a bad 'un! he's a bad 'un! he's an out-and-outer!"

"Do you know which of them struck the captain down?"

"He did," he answered at once.

"I could have sworn it by the way in which he excused the murderer."

"Stevens," continued the boatswain, "is at the bottom of all this here business—him and the cook. I suppose he didn't want the cook for a chum, and so knocked him over when he was going to operate on Duckling's body. But Duckling was a bad 'un too, and so was the skipper. They've got to thank theirselves for what they48 got. The crew never would ha' turned had they been properly fed."

"I believe that," I said. "But I'll tell you what's troubling me, boatswain. The carpenter has some design behind all this, which he is concealing. Does he really mean that I should navigate the ship to within fifty miles of New Orleans?"

"Yes, sir, he do," answered the boatswain, regarding me stedfastly.

"And he means then to heave the ship to, lower away the boats, and make for one of the mouths of the Mississippi, or land upon some part of the coast, and represent himself and his companions as castaway sailors?"

"Quite right," said the boatswain, watching me fixedly.

"If that is really his intention," I proceeded, "I cannot believe that he will allow me to land with the others. He distrusts49 me. He is as suspicious as all murderers are."

The boatswain continued eyeing me intently, as a man might who strives to form a resolution from the expression in another's face.

"He means to scuttle the ship," he said, in a low voice.

"Ah!" I exclaimed, starting. "I should have foreseen this."

"He means to scuttle her just before he puts off in the boats," he added in a whisper.

I watched him anxiously, for I saw that he had more to tell me. He looked up at both skylights, then towards the cuddy door, then towards the companion ladder, bent over to me, and said—

"Mr. Royle, he don't mean to let you leave this vessel."

"He means to scuttle her, leaving me on board?"

50 He nodded.

"Did he tell you this?"

He nodded again.

"When?"

"Just now."

"And them?" I exclaimed, pointing towards the cabin in which were Mr. Robertson and his daughter.

"They'll be left too," he replied.

I took a deep breath, and closed the knife and fork on my plate.

"Now then, mate!" bawled the carpenter's voice, down the companion; "how long are you goin' to be?"

"Coming," answered the boatswain.

A thought had flashed upon me.

"There must be others in this ship whom Stevens distrusts as well as me," I whispered. "Who are they? Give me but two other men and yourself, and I'll engage that the ship will be ours! See! if these51 men whom he distrusts could be told that, at the last moment, they will be left to sink in a scuttled ship, they would come over on my side to save their lives. How are they to be got at?"

He shook his head without speaking, and left the table; but turned to say, "Don't be in a hurry. I've got two hours afore me, and I'll turn it over." He then went on deck.

I remained at the cuddy table, buried in thought. The boatswain's communication had utterly taken me by surprise. That Stevens, after the promise he had made me that there should be no more bloodshed, after the sympathy I had shown the men from the beginning, should be base enough to determine upon murdering me and the inoffensive persons we had rescued, at the moment when we might think our escape from our heavy misfortunes certain, was so52 shocking that the thought of it made me feel as one stunned. An emotion of deep despair was bred in me, and then this, in its turn, begot a wild fit of fury. I could scarcely restrain myself from rushing on deck and shooting the ruffian as he stood there.

To escape from my own insanity, I ran into the captain's cabin, and locked the door, and plunged into deep and bitter reflection.

It was idle for me to think of resistance in my then condition. Upon whom could I count? The boatswain? I could not be sure that he would aid me single-handed, nor hope that he would try to save my life at the risk of his own. The steward? Such a feeble-hearted creature would only hamper me, would be of less use even than old Mr. Robertson. Many among the crew, if not all of them indeed, must obviously be53 acquainted with Stevens' murderous intentions, and would make a strong and desperate gang to oppose me; and though I should discover the men who were not in the carpenter's confidence, how could I depend on them at the last moment?

The feeling of helplessness induced in me by these considerations was profound and annihilating. I witnessed the whole murderous process as though it were happening: the ship hove to, the boats shoving away, one, perhaps, remaining to watch the vessel sink, that they might be in no doubt of our having perished. All this would happen in the dark too, for the departure of the men from the ship would only be safe at night, that no passing vessel might espy them.

An idea that will sound barbarous, though I should not have hesitated to carry it out could I have seen my way to it, occurred to54 me. This was to watch an opportunity when the carpenter was alone, to hurl him overboard. But here, again, the chances against me were fifty to one. To destroy the villain without risk of detection, without the act being witnessed, without suspicion attaching to me on his being missed, would imply such a host of favouring conditions as the kindliest fortune could scarcely assemble together.

What then was to be done?

I had already pointed out the course the ship was to steer, and could not alter it. But though I should plausibly alter her course a point or two, what could follow? The moment land was sighted, let it be what coast it would, they would know I had deceived them; or, giving me the credit of having mistaken my reckonings, they would heave the ship to themselves, and then would come the dastardly crime. I dared55 not signal any passing vessel. Let my imagination devise what it would, it could invent nothing that my judgment would adopt; since, being single-handed in this ship, no effort I could make to save the lives of the persons it was my determination to stand by, but must end in our destruction.

By such confessions I show myself no hero; but then I do not want to be thought one. I was, and am, a plain man, placed in one of the most formidable situations that any one could find himself in. In the darkness and horror of that time I saw no means of escape, and so I admit my blindness. A few strokes of the pen would easily show me other than I was, but then I should not be telling the truth, and should be falsely taking glory to myself, instead of truly showing it to be God's, by whose mercy I am alive to tell the story.

56 My clothes and other things belonging to me being in the cabin now occupied by Stevens, I opened the door and desired the steward to bring them to me. My voice was heard by Miss Robertson, who came round the table to where I stood, and thanked me for my kindness to her and her father.

She had made good use of the few conveniences I had been able to send her. Her hair was brushed, and most prettily looped over the comb, and she wore a collar that became her mightily, which she had found in the steward's box. She looked a sweet and true English girl; her deathlike pallor gradually yielding to a healthy white with a tinge of colour on the cheeks.

"Papa seems better," she said, "and is constantly asking for you; but I told him," (with the prettiest smile,) "that you require rest as well as others, and that you have plenty to occupy you."

Then looking earnestly at me for some moments, while her face grew wonderfully grave, she exclaimed—

"What is wrong, Mr. Royle? What makes you look so anxious and worried?"

"There is plenty to trouble me," I answered, not carelessly, but not putting too much significance into my tone, for at that moment I did not think I ought to tell her the truth. "You know the men have mutinied, and that my position is a difficult one. I have to be careful how I act, both for my sake and yours."

"Yes, I know that," she said, keeping her clear and thoughtful eyes on me. "But then you said you did not fear that the men would be violent again, and that they would leave us on board this ship when we were near New Orleans."

I watched her face some time without speaking, asking myself if I should take her into my confidence, if I ought to impart the diabolical scheme of Stevens, as told me by the boatswain. Certainly I should have put her off without telling her the truth had not the courageous expression in her eyes, her firm and beautiful mouth, her resolute voice and manner, told me she would know how to bear it.

"I will not conceal that I have heard something just now which has affected me very much," I said to her. "Will you step into my cabin? We can talk there without being seen," I added, having observed Stevens walk along the main-deck, and expecting that he would return in a few moments to his cabin, it being his watch below.

She followed me in silence, and I closed the door.

"I will tell you in a few words," I at once began, "what I heard just now. I told the boatswain that I questioned whether the men would let me land with them for fear of the evidence I could give. He replied that he had gathered from the carpenter, while at breakfast, that the men intended to scuttle the ship when they quitted her, and to leave us on board."

"To drown?"

"That is their idea."

She pursed up her mouth tightly, and pressed her hand to her forehead. That was all. Whatever emotion my statement inspired was hidden. She said in a low voice—

"They are fiends! I did not think them so cruel—my poor father!"

"This is what I am told they mean to do; and I know Stevens to be a ruffian, and that he will carry out his project if he can. I have spent some time alone here, in trying to think how we can save ourselves; as yet I see no remedy. But wait," I said; "it will take us three weeks, sailing well every day, to reach the Gulf of Mexico. I have this time before me; and in that time not only something must, but something shall be done."

She did not answer.

"I will hazard nothing. I will venture no risks; what I resolve to do must be effectual," I went on, "because my life is dearer to me now than it was three days ago, for your and your father's sake. You must be saved from these ruffians, but no risk must attend your deliverance. That is why I see no escape before us as yet; but it will come—it will come! Despair is very fruitful in expedients, and I am not beaten because I find myself flung like a dog in a hole!"

She looked up at this, and said, "What is to be done?"

61 "I must think."

"I will think, too. We need not tell papa?" she added, toning her voice to a question, with an appealing look in her eyes.

"No, certainly not. Remember, we are not supposed to question the men's honest intentions towards us. We must appear utterly ignorant."

"Are they armed?" she inquired.

"No."

She cast her eyes round the cabin and said, "Have you no guns?"

"Nothing but a pistol. But though we had twenty guns we have no hands to use them. So far as I know as yet, there is no man who would stand with me—not even the boatswain, unless he were sure we should conquer the ruffians."

"Could I not use a pistol? Ah, I remember, you have only one."

62 She sank her chin on her hand and looked downwards, lost in thought.

"Why would you not steer the ship for some near port?" she asked presently.

"I could not alter the course without being challenged. Remember that my policy is not to excite suspicion of my honesty."

"If a gale would rise like that which wrecked the Cecilia, it might drive us near the land, where we could get help."

"No, we shall have to depend upon ourselves. I do not want to pin my faith on chance."

I began to pace to and fro, torn by the blind and useless labours of my mind.

Just then a step sounded along the cuddy. The cabin door was pushed open roughly, and Stevens walked in. He stared at Miss Robertson, and cried—

"Sorry to interrupt. Didn't know you63 was here, mam, I'm sure. I thought," addressing me, "I should find you turned in. I've come to have a look at that chart o' yours. How long d'ye make it to New Orleans?"

"About three weeks."

"Well, there's live stock enough for three weeks, any ways. I've just told the cook to stick one of them porkers. All hands has a fancy for roast pork to-day. Sarvant, miss. You was pretty nigh drownded, I think."

"My father and I owe our lives to the noble fellows in this ship. They must be brave and good men to risk their lives to save ours," she answered, with a smile of touching sweetness, looking frankly into the face of the miscreant who stood, cap on head, before her.

"Lor' bless yer!" he exclaimed; "there wasn't no risk. I'd ha' swum the distance in such a sea for five shilling."

64 She shook her head with another smile (I judged the effort this piece of acting cost her), as she said—

"I know that English sailors always undervalue their good deeds. But happily my father is a rich man, and when you land us he will take care that no man on board this ship shall complain of his gratitude."

"Oh, he's rich!" exclaimed the carpenter, as though struck with a new idea.

"Very rich."

"How rich might he be, mam?"

"Well, he owned the ship that you saved us from—cargo and ship."

14

She could not have offered a better illustration of her father's wealth to the man, for he would appreciate the value of a vessel of that size.

"And what do you think he'll give the men—them as saved him, I suppose?"

"Oh, he won't make any difference. He is indebted to you all, for I have heard that the captain would not have stopped for us had he not been obliged to do so by the crew."

"That's true enough," rejoined the carpenter with an oath, looking at me.

"Perfectly true," I made haste to say.

"My father would not certainly offer less than one hundred pounds to each man," she said quite simply.

He pulled off his cap at this and twirled it and let it drop; picked it up so slowly that I thought he would never bend his body sufficiently to enable him to recover it; looked at her sideways as he put it on his head again, and then said to me with offensive abruptness—

"Come, master, let's have a look at that blooming chart."

I opened the door to let Miss Robertson pass out, exchanging one glance with her as she left, and addressed myself to the carpenter.

He pored over the chart with his dirty forefinger upon it.

"Whereabouts are we now?" he inquired.

I pointed to the spot as near as I could judge from yesterday's reckonings.

"What's this here line?" he asked.

"That's the longitude."

He ran his eye to the bottom of the chart and exclaimed—

"Thirty. Is that it?"

"Call it thirty."

"But what do you call it?"

"Thirty, I tell you—thirty degrees west longitude."

"And this here line's the latitude, I suppose?"

"Yes."

"That's forty."

"Call it forty-four."

"Will that make it right?"

"Pretty nearly."

"What are all these here dots and streaks?" said he, after squinting with his nose close to the chart. "Blowed if ever I could read them small words."

"They are the Azores."

"Oh, we're to the norrards o' them, aren't we?" he inquired sharply.

"You can see for yourself," I answered, putting my finger on the chart.

"Where's this blessed Gulf of Mexico?" he inquired, after casting his eyes all over the chart.

"There."

He ran his dirty thumbnail in a line to the the Gulf, and asked me what that blot was.

"Bermuda."

"You'll keep south o' that, will yer?"

"If I can, certainly."

"It's a man-o'-war station, I've heerd."

"I believe it is."

"All right," he said, and looking at the boat's compass on the table, asked if it were true.

I told him it was; whereupon he set it on the chart and compared its indications with the line he had run down the chart, and was going away, when I said—

"What do you think of the young lady's idea? I should like to earn a hundred pounds."

"So should I," he answered gruffly, pausing.

"It would pretty well pay me for what I have had to put up with from Coxon."

He gave me an indescribable look, full of fierceness, suspicion, and cunning.

"I dessay it would, if you got it," he said, and walked out, banging the door after him.

CHAPTER III.

I had been greatly struck by the firmness with which Miss Robertson had received the ghastly bit of information I gave her, and not more by this than by her gentle and genial manner towards the carpenter, wherein she had shown herself perfectly well qualified to act with me in this critical, dangerous time. She had only just been rescued from one trial frightful enough in character to have driven one, at least, of the male sufferers mad; and now fate had plunged her into a worse situation, and yet she could confront the terrors of it calmly, and deliberate collectedly upon the danger.

Such a character as this was, I thought, of the true type of heroine, with nothing in it that was strained; calm in emergency, and with a fruitful mind scattering hope around it—even though no more than hope—as the teeming flower sheds its perfume. I had especially noticed the quickness with which she had conceived and expressed that idea about her father rewarding the men; it inspirited me, in spite of the reception Stevens had given it. One hundred pounds a man was a promise that might move them into a very different train of thought from what Stevens had induced and was sustaining.

Having heard the carpenter enter his cabin, I determined to step on deck and take the boatswain's sense on this new idea. But before quitting the cuddy, I knocked lightly on Miss Robertson's cabin door.

She opened it instantly.

"Will you come on deck?" I asked her.

"Yes, if I can be of use there."

"The air will refresh you after your confinement to this cabin, and will do your father good."

"He is sleeping now," she answered, opening the door fully, that I might see the old man.

"Let him sleep," said I; "that will do him more good. But you will come?"

"Yes, with pleasure."

"You have nothing to fear from the men," I said, wishing to reassure her. "They are willing to acknowledge the authority of the persons they have put over them—the bo'sun, Stevens, and myself."

"I should not mind if they spoke to me," she exclaimed. "I should know what to say to them, unless they were brutal."

She suddenly added, putting her hand to her head, and almost laughing—

"I have no hat."

"I have a straw hat you shall have," I said, and brought it.

She put it on her head, and it sat very well on the pile of yellow hair that lay heaped over her comb.

"How strange," she said, speaking in the whisper in which our conversation had been carried on, "to find oneself destitute,—without even the commonest necessaries! When the captain of the Cecilia said we were sinking, papa ran with me out of the cabin. We did not think of putting on our hats, nor of saving anything but our lives."

She turned to look at her father, closed the door tenderly, and accompanied me on deck.

The morning was now advanced. The day was still very bright; and the wonderful blue of the heavens lost nothing of its richness from contrast with the stately and swelling clouds—pearl-coloured where they faced the sun, and with here and there a rainbow on their skirts, and centres of creamy white—which sailed solemnly over it.

The breeze had freshened, but the swell had greatly subsided, and the sea was almost smooth, with brilliant little waves chasing it. The ship was stretching finely along the water, all sail set and every sail drawing.

On our lee beam was the canvas of a big ship, her hull invisible; and astern of her I could just make out the faint tracing of the smoke of a steamer upon the sky. The sun shone warm, but not too warm; the strong breeze was sweet and soft; the ship's motion steady, and her aspect a glorious picture of white and rounded canvas, taut rigging delicately interlaced, and gleaming decks and glittering brass-work. The blue water sang a racing chorus at the bows, and the echo died upon the broad and bubbling wake astern.

I ran my eye forwards upon the men on the forecastle. Most of the crew were congregated there, lounging, squatting, smoking—no man doing any work. I wondered, not at this, but that they should be so orderly and keep their place. They might have come aft had they pleased, swarmed into the cuddy, occupied the cabins; for the ship was theirs. Since they acted with so much decency, could they not be won over from their leader's atrocious project? If I went among them, holding this girl, now at my side, by the hand, and pleaded for her life, if not for my own, would they not spare her? would not some among them be moved by her beauty and her helplessness?

Nothing should seem more rational than such conjectures, always providing that I ceased to remember these men were criminals, that their one idea now was to elude the law, and that I who should plead, and those for whom I pleaded, could by a word, when set on shore, procure the conviction of the whole gang, charge them with their crimes, prove their identity, and secure their punishment. Would not Stevens keep them in mind of this? Knowing what they knew, knowing what they meditated, I say that in the very orderliness of their behaviour, I witnessed something more sinister than I should have found in violent conduct. I alone could carry them to where they wished to go. I must be conciliated, pleased, obeyed, and my fears tranquillized. If I failed them, their doom was inevitable; shipwreck or capture was certain. All this was plain to me as the fingers on my hand; and during the brief time I stood watching them, I found myself repeating again and again the hopeless question, "What can I do?"

Miss Robertson seated herself on one of the skylights, that nearest the break of the poop. The boatswain glanced at her respectfully, and the men forward stared, and some of them laughed, but none of the remarks they indulged in were audible.

Fish was at the wheel. I went to the binnacle, and said—

"That's our course. Let this wind hold, and we'll soon be clear of this mess."

"Three weeks about, I gives us," answered the man.

"And long enough, too," said I.

He spat the quid in his mouth overboard, and dried his lips on his cuff. As he did not seem disposed to talk, I left him and joined the boatswain, and at my request he came and stood with me near Miss Robertson.

77 "I have told this lady what you repeated to me at breakfast," I said, in a low voice. "She is full of courage, and I have asked her to come on deck that we may talk before her."

"If she's as brave as she's pretty, I reckon not many 'll carry stouter hearts in 'em than her," he said, addressing her full, with an air of respectful gallantry that was very taking.

She looked down with a smile.

"Boatswain," said I, "every hour is precious to us, for at any moment Stevens may change the ship's course for a closer shore than the American; and though we should hold on for the Gulf, it may take us all our time to hit on a scheme to save ourselves and work it out. I have come to tell you an idea suggested by this lady, Miss Robertson. Her father is a rich man, owner of the vessel he was wrecked in——"

78 "Robertson and Co., of Liverpool, ship-brokers?" he interrupted, addressing her.

"Yes," she replied.

"Why, I sailed in one o' that firm's wessels as bo'sun's mate, three year ago, the Albany she was called, and a werry comfortable ship she was, well found and properly commanded."

"Indeed!" she exclaimed, brightening up and looking at him eagerly. And then, reflecting a little, she said—"The Albany—that ship was commanded by Captain Tribett."

"Quite right, miss, Tribett was the name. And the first mate's name was Green, and the second's Gull, and the third—ah! he were Captain Tribett's son,—same name of course. Well, blow me if this ain't wot the Italians calls a cohincidence."

He was as pleased as she, and stood grinning on her.

79 "Mr. Royle," she exclaimed, raising her fine eyes to mine, "surely there must be others like the boatswain in this ship. They cannot all be after the pattern of that horrible carpenter!"

"We ought to be able to find that out, bos'un," I said.

"Look here, miss," he answered, with a glance first at the men forward and then at Fish at the wheel, "the circumstances of this here affair is just this: the crew have been very badly treated, fed with rotten stores, and starved and abused by the skipper and chief mate until they went mad. I don't think myself that they meant to kill the captain and Mr. Duckling; but it happened, and no man barrin' Stevens was guiltier than his mate, and that's where it is. The carpenter knocked the skipper down, and others kicked him when he was down, not knowing he was dead; and four80 or five set on Mr. Duckling, and so you see it's a sin as they all share alike in. If one man had killed the skipper, and another man had killed the chief mate, why then so be, miss, the others might be got to turn upon 'em to save their own necks. But here it's all hands as did the job. And the only man who kept away, though I pretended to be one with 'em hearty enough, was me; and wot's the consequince. Stevens don't trust me; and I'm sartin in my own mind that he don't mean to let me into the boats when the time comes, any more than you."

So saying, he deliberately walked aft, looked at the compass, then at the sails, and patrolled the poop for several minutes, for the very obvious reason that the men should not take notice of our talking long and close together.

Presently he rejoined us, standing a little distance away, and in a careless attitude.

81 "Bo'sun," said I, addressing him with my eyes on the deck, so that from a distance I would not appear to be speaking, "Miss Robertson told Stevens that her father

would handsomely reward every man on board this ship on her arrival in port. He asked her what her father would give, and she said a hundred pounds to each man. If this were repeated to the crew, what effect would it produce?"

"They wouldn't believe it."

"My father would give each man a promise in writing," she exclaimed.

"They wouldn't trust him," said the boatswain, without reflecting. "They'd think it a roose to bring 'em together to give 'em into custody. If I was one of them that's what I should think, and you may be sure I'm right."

"But he would give them written orders on his bankers; they could not think it a 82 ruse," she said eagerly, evidently enamoured of her own idea, since she saw that I entertained it.

"Sailors don't no nothing about banks and the likes of that, miss. There are thirteen men in the ship's company, counting the cook and the steward. Call 'em twelve. If your father had a bag of sovereigns on board this wessel, and counted out a hundred to each man, then they'd believe him. But I'd not believe them. They'd take the money and scuttle the ship all the same. Don't make no mistake. They're fond o' their wagabone lives, and the carpenter's given 'em such a talkin' to, that they're precious keen on gettin' away and cuttin' off all evidence. It 'ud take more than a hundred pound each man to make 'em willing to risk their lives."

He walked away once more and stood lounging aft, chatting with Fish.

83 "I am afraid the bo'sun is right," said I. "Having lived among them and heard their conversation, he would know their characters too well to be deceived in the consequences of your scheme."

"But papa would pay them, Mr. Royle. He would give them any pledge they might choose to name, that they would run no risk. The money could be sent to them—they need not appear—they need not be seen."

"We know they would run no risks; but could we get them to believe us?"

"At least let us try."

"No—forgive me—we must not try. We must have nothing more to say. You have spoken to Stevens; let him talk among the men. If the reward tempt them, be sure they will concert measures among themselves to land you. But I beg you to have no faith in this project. They are villains, who will betray you in the end. 84 The boatswain's arguments respecting them are perfectly just—so just that he has inspired me with a new kind of faith in him. He owns that his own life is in jeopardy, and I believe he will hit upon some expedient to save us. See how he watches us! He will join us presently. I, too, have a scheme dawning in my head, but too imperfect to discuss as yet. Courage!" I said, animated by her beauty and the deep, speaking expression of her blue eyes: "the bo'sun's confession of his own danger makes me feel stronger by a man. I have greater confidence in him than I had. If I could but muster a few firearms—for even the steward might be made a man of, fighting for his life with a revolver in his hand—there is nothing I would not dare. But twelve to two!—what is our chance? It must not be thought of, with you and your father depending for your lives on ours."

85 "No," she answered firmly. "There must be other and better ways. I will think as well as you."

The boatswain came sauntering towards us. He flung a coil of rope over a belaying-pin, looked over the ship's side, approached us nearer, and pulled out a pipe and asked me for a light. I had one in my pocket and gave it to him. This was his excuse to speak.

"It isn't so suspicious lookin' to talk now as it would be at night or in the cuddy—and in the cuddy there's no telling whose ears are about," he said. "I'll give you my

19

scheme, thought on since breakfast, and listen close, for I durstn't talk much; after this we must belay, or the men 'll be set jawing. When we come to the Gulf of Mexico, you'll let me know how long it'll be afore we're fifty mile off the Mississippi. I helped to stow the cargo in this vessel, and86 she's choke full, and there's only one place as they'll be able to get at to scuttle her, and that's right forrards of the fore hatch. I'll let that out to Stevens bit by bit, in an ordinary way, and he'll remember it. The night afore we heave to—you'll tell me when—I'll fall overboard and get drowned. That'll happen in your watch. We'll get one o' them packin' cases full o' tin-tack up out o' the steerage and stow it away in one of the quarter-boats, and you'll let that drop overboard, d'ye see? which 'll sound like a man's body, and sink right away, and then you'll roar out that the boatswain's fallen overboard. Let 'em do what they like. I shall be stowed away forrard, down in the forepeak somewheers, and the man as comes there to bore a hole, I'll choke. Leave the rest to me. If Stevens he sings out to know if it's done, I'll say 'Yes,' and tell him to lower away the boats, and hold on for me.87 He'll take my voice for the fellow as is scuttling the ship. Now," he added vehemently, "I'll lay any man fifty pound agin ten shillings, that Stevens don't wait for the man he sends below. He'll get into the boat and shove off and lay by. You'll give me the signal, and I'll come up sharp, an' if there's a breath o' air we'll have the mainyards round somehow; and if the boats get in our road we'll run 'em down; and if there's no wind, and they try to board us—let 'em look out! for there'll be more blood-letting among 'em than ever they saw before, by God!"

He motioned with his hand that we should leave the poop, and walked away.

Miss Robertson looked at me and I at her for some moments in silence.

"Will it do, Mr. Royle?" she asked, in a low voice.

"Yes," I said.

88 "You think we shall be saved by this stratagem?"

I reflected before answering, and then said, "I do."

She went down the companion-ladder, and when we were in the cuddy, she took my hand in both of hers, and pressed it tightly to her heart, then hurried into her cabin.

89

CHAPTER IV.

The more I considered the boatswain's proposal, the better I liked it. All that day I turned it over and over in my mind. And, what was useful to me, I could sleep when I lay down in my watches below, which was a luxury I had feared, after the boatswain's disclosure at the breakfast-table, would be denied me.

I did not wish Miss Robertson to sit at the cuddy table at meal hours, and when dinner-time came I took care that as good a meal should be taken to her and her father as the ship could furnish.

When Stevens joined me at the table, he90 sang out to the steward to "tell the old gent an' his darter that dinner vos a vaitin'!" Whereupon I explained that the old gentleman was too ill to leave his bunk.

"Well, then, let the gal come," said he.

"She can't leave her father," I replied.

"Perhaps it ain't that so much as because I ain't genteel enough for her. It's the vest end o' London as won't have nothen to do with Wapping. The tobaccy in my breath's too strong for her."

"Nothing of the kind. The old man is ill, and she must watch him. As to your manners, I dare say she is better pleased with them than you ought to be told. It is not every ship's carpenter that could talk and look like a skipper, and keep men under as you do."

"You're right there!" he exclaimed, with a broad grin. "Come, sarve us out a dollop91 o' that pork, will yer? Roast pork's never too fresh for me."

And he fell like an animal to the meat, and forgot, as I wished, all about Miss Robertson.

In the first watch, from eight in the evening until midnight, which was the boatswain's, I went and sat for an hour with the old gentleman and his daughter. Not a word was said about the peril we were in; he was quite ignorant of it, and, being better and stronger, was eager in his questions about the ship's progress.

I took notice that he appeared to forget all about the mutiny, and conversed as if I were captain. Nor did he show any strong recollection of the loss of his ship and the circumstances attending it. Indeed, it seemed that as he grew better his memory grew worse. That was the faculty injured by his sufferings, and when I listened to his92 questions, which took no cognizance of things of the past, though as recent as yesterday, I thought his memory would presently quit him wholly, for he was an old man, with a mind too feeble to hold on tightly.

I left them at half-past nine, and went on deck. I tried to see who was at the wheel, but could not make the man out. I think it was one of the Dutchmen. Better this man than Fish, Johnson, or some of the others, whose names I forget, who were thick with the carpenter, and before whom it would not be wise to talk with any suggestion of mystery with the boatswain.

However, there was not much chance of my being noticed, for the night was gloomy, and all about the decks quite dark. The ship was under topsails and main topgallant sail; the wind was east-south-east, blowing freshly, with long seas. There was no appearance of foul weather, and the glass93 stood steady; but an under-sky of level cloud lay stretched across the stars; and looking abroad over the ship's side, nothing was distinguishable but the foam of the waves breaking as they ran.

As I emerged from the companion, the boatswain hailed the forecastle, and told the man there to keep a good look-out. I had not had an opportunity of speaking to him since the morning. I touched him on the arm, and he turned and stared to see who I was.

"Ah, Mr. Royle," said he.

"Let's get under the lee of that quarter-boat," said I. "We can hear each other there. Who's at the wheel?"

"Dutch Joe."

"Come to the binnacle first, and I'll talk to you about the ship's course, and then we'll get under the quarter-boat, and he'll think I am giving you sailing directions."

94 We did this, and I gave the boatswain some instructions in the hearing of the Dutchman; and to appear very much in earnest, the boatswain and I hove the log whilst Dutch Joe turned the glass, which he could easily attend to, holding a spoke with one hand, for the ship was steering herself.

We then walked to the quarter-boat and stood under the lee of it.

"Bo'sun," said I, "the more I think of your scheme, the better I like it. Whatever may happen, your being in the hold will prevent any man from scuttling the ship."

"Yes, so it will; I'll take care of that. One blow must do the job—he mustn't cry out. The pianofortes are amidships on nearly two foot of dunnage; all forrard the cases run large, and it's there they'll find space."

"My intention is not to wait until we95 come to the Gulf in order to carry this out," said I; "I'll clap on sixty, eighty, a hundred miles, just as I see my way, to every day's run, so as to bring the Gulf of Mexico close alongside the Bermuda Islands. Do you understand, bo'sun?"

"Yes, I understand. There's no use in waitin'. You're quite right to get it over. The sooner the better, says I."

"We shall average a run of 300 miles every twenty-four hours, and I'll slip in an extra degree whenever I can. Who's to know?"

"Ne'er a man on this wessel, sir," he answered. "There's not above two as can spell words in a book."

"So I should think. Of course I shall have to prick off the chart according to the wind. A breeze like this may well give us three hundred miles. If it fall calm I can make her drift sixty miles west-sou'-west,96 and clap on another eighty for steerage way. I shall have double reckonings—one for the crew, one for myself. You, as chief mate, will know it's all right."

"Leave that to me," he answered, with a short laugh. "They've found out by this time that the ship's a clipper, and I'll let 'em understand that there never was a better navigator than you. It 'll be for you and me to keep as much canvas on her as she'll carry in our watches, for the sake of appearance; and if I was you, sir, I'd trim the log-line afresh."

"A good idea," said I. "I'll give her a double dose. Twelve knots shall be nothing in a moderate breeze."

We both laughed at this; and then, to make my presence on deck appear reasonable, I walked to the binnacle.

I returned and said—

"In nine days hence we must contrive to97 be in longitude 62° and latitude 33°;—somewhere about it. If we can average 180 miles every day we shall do it."

"What do you make the distance from where we are now to the Gulf?"

"In broad numbers, three thousand miles."

"No more?"

"Averaging two hundred miles a day we should be abreast of New Orleans in a fortnight. I said three weeks, but I shall correct myself to Stevens to-morrow, after I have taken observations. I'll show him a jump on the chart that will astonish him. I'll punish the scoundrels yet. I'll give them the direct course to Bermuda when they're in the boats, and if our plot only succeeds and the wind serves, one of us two will be ashore on the island before them, to let the governor know whom he is to expect."

98 "That may be done, too," answered the boatswain; "but it'll have to be a dark night to get away from 'em without their seeing of us."

"They'll choose a dark night for their own sakes. Boatswain, give us your hand. Your cleverness has in my opinion as good as saved us. I felt a dead man this morning, but I never was more alive, thanks to you, than I am now."

I grasped his hand, and went below, positively in better spirits that I had enjoyed since I first put my foot upon this ill-fated ship.

*****

The first thing I did next morning was to mark off the log-line afresh, having smuggled the reel below during my watch. I shortened the distances between the knots considerably, so that a greater number should pass over the stern whilst the sand99 was running than would be reeled off if the line were true.

At eight bells, when the boatswain went on deck, I asked him to take the log with him; and following him presently, just as Stevens was about to leave the poop, I looked around me, as if studying the weather, and exclaimed—

"Bos'un, you must keep the log going, please. Heave it every hour, never less. I may have to depend upon dead-reckoning to-day, Mr. Stevens;" and I pointed to the sky, which was as thick as it had been all night.

"Shall I heave it now?" inquired the boatswain.

"Did you heave it in your watch, Mr. Stevens?" said I.

"No," he replied. "What are we doin' now? This has been her pace all along—ha'n't touched a brace or given an order since I came on deck."

100 He had come on deck to relieve me at four.

"Let's heave the log," I exclaimed; "I shall be better satisfied."

I gave the glass to Stevens, and whilst arranging the log-ship, I looked over the side, and said—

"By Jove, she's walking and no mistake."

"I allow that we're doing ten," said the man at the wheel.

"I give her thirteen good," said I.

"Call it fifteen, and you'll not be far out," observed the boatswain.

The carpenter cocked his evil eye at the water, but hazarded no conjecture.

"She can sail—if she can't do nothen else," was all he said.

I flung the log-ship overboard.

"Turn!" I cried out.

I saw the knots fibbing out like a string of beads. The reel roared in the boatswain's hands, and when Stevens called101 "Stop!" I caught the line and allowed it to jam me against the rail, as though the weight of it, dragged through the water at the phenomenal speed at which we were supposed to be going, would haul me overboard.

"What's that knot there, Mr. Stevens?" I called out. "Bear a hand! the line is cutting my fingers in halves!"

He put down the sand-glass and laid hold of the line where the knot was, and began to count.

"Fifteen!" he roared.

"Well, I'm jiggered!" exclaimed the man steering.

I looked at Stevens triumphantly, as though I should say, "What do you think of that?"

"I told you you wur wrong, Mr. Royle," said the boatswain. "It's all fifteen. By jingo! it ain't sailing, it's engine drivin'!"

102 The true speed of the Grosvenor was about nine and a half knots—certainly not more; and whether the carpenter should believe the report of the log or not, was nothing to me.

"Log it fifteen on the slate, bo'sun, and keep the log going every hour," I said, and went below again.

I saw, as was now my regular custom at every meal, that the steward took a good breakfast to the Robertsons' cabin, and then sat down with Stevens to the morning repast.

I took this opportunity of suggesting that if the wind held, and the vessel maintained her present rate of speed, we might hope to be in the Gulf of Mexico in a fortnight.

"How do you make that out? It was three weeks yesterday."

"And it might have been a month," I answered. "But a few days of this kind of103 sailing, let me tell you, Mr. Stevens, make a great difference in one's calculations."

"How fur off is the Gulf of Mexico?" he asked.

"About a couple of thousand miles."

"Oh, a couple of thousand miles. Well, an' what reckoning do you get out o' that?"

"Suppose you put the ship's pace down at thirteen knots an hour?"

"I thought you made it fifteen?" he exclaimed, looking at me suspiciously.

"Yes, but I don't suppose we shall keep that up. For the sake of argument I call it thirteen?"

"Well?" cramming his mouth as he spoke.

"In twenty-four hours we shall have run a distance of three hundred and twelve miles."

He nodded.

"Therefore, if we have the luck to keep up this pace of two knots less than we are now actually doing, for fifteen days, we shall have accomplished—let me see."

I drew out a pencil, and commenced a calculation on the back of an old envelope.

"Three hundred and twelve multiplied by fifteen. Five times naught are naught; three naughts and two are ten; add two thousand; we shall have accomplished a distance of four thousand six hundred and eighty miles—that is two thousand six hundred and eighty miles further than we want to go."

He was puzzled (and well he might be) by my fluent figures, but would not appear so.

"I understand," said he.

"Stop a bit," I exclaimed; "I want to show you something."

I entered the captain's cabin, procured a chart of the North and South Atlantic, including the eastern American coast, and spread it upon the table.

"The two thousand miles I have given you," said I, "would bring you right off the Mississippi. See here."

He rose and stooped over the chart.

"The short cut to the Gulf," I continued, pointing with my pencil, "is through the Florida Channel, clean through the Bahamas, where the navigation is very ugly."

"I see."

"I wouldn't trust myself there without a pilot on any consideration, and, of course," said I, looking at him, "we don't want a pilot."

"I should rayther think we don't," he answered, scowling at the chart.

"So," I went on, "to keep clear of ships and boats, which are sure to board us if we get among these islands, I should steer round the Caribees, do you see?—well away from them, and up through the Caribbean Sea, into the Gulf. Do you follow me?"

"Yes, yes—I see."

"Now, Mr. Stevens," said I very gravely, "I want to do my duty to the crew, and put them and myself in the way of getting ashore and clear off from all bad consequences."

The scoundrel tried to meet my eyes, but could not; and he listened to me, gazing the while on the chart.

"But I don't think I should succeed if I got among those islands blocking up the entrance of the Gulf; and as to the Gulf itself, you may take your oath it's full of ships, some of which will pick you up before you reach the shore, whilst others are pretty certain to come across the vessel you have abandoned, and then—look out!"

He swallowed some coffee hastily, stared at the chart, and said in a surly voice, "What are you drivin' at?"

"Instead of our abandoning the ship in the Gulf of Mexico," I said, "my opinion is that, in order to assure our safety, and lessen the chance of detection, we ought to abandon her clear of these islands, to the norrard of them, off this coast here—Florida," pointing to the chart.

"You think so?" he said, doubtfully, after a long pause.

"I am certain of it. We ought to land upon some uninhabited part of the coast, travel along it northwards, until we reach a town, and there represent ourselves as shipwrecked sailors. Ask your mates if I am not right."

"Perhaps you are," he replied, still very dubious, though not speaking distrustfully.

"If you select the coast of Florida, clear of all these islands, and away from the track of ships, I'll undertake, with good winds, to put the ship off it in nine or ten days. But I'll not answer for our safety if you oblige me to navigate her into the Gulf of Mexico."

He continued looking at the chart for some moments, and I saw by the movements of his lips that he was trying to spell the names of the places written on the Florida coast outline, though he would not ask me to help him.

At last he said—

"It's Fish and two others as chose New Orleans. I have no fancy for them half-an'-half places. What I wanted was to get away into the Gulf of Guinea, and coast along down to Congo, or that way. I know that coast, but I never was in Amerikey, and," he added, fetching the chart a blow with his fist, "curse me if I like the notion of going there."

"It won't do to be shifting about," said I, frightened that he would go and get the crew to agree with him to run down to the African coast, which would seriously prolong the journey, and end, for all I could tell, in defeating my scheme; "we shall be running short of water and eatable stores, and then we shall be in a fix. Make up your mind, Mr. Stevens, to the Florida coast; you can't do better. We shall fetch it in a few days, and once ashore, we can disperse in parties, and each party can tell their own yarn if they are asked questions."

"Well, I'll talk to Fish and the others about it," he growled, going back to his seat. "I think you're right about them West Indie Islands. We must keep clear o' them. Perhaps some of 'em forrards may know what this here Florida is like. I was never ashore there."

He fell to his breakfast again, and finding him silent, and considering that enough had been said for the present, I left him.

I did not know how well I had argued the matter until that night, when he came to me on the poop, at half-past eight, and told me that the men were all agreed that it would be too dangerous to abandon the ship off New Orleans, and that they preferred the notion of leaving her off the Florida coast.

I asked him if I was to consider this point definitely settled, and on his answering in the affirmative, I sang out to the man at the wheel to keep her away a couple of points, and ordered some of the watch to haul in a bit on the weather braces, explaining to Stevens that his decision would bring our course a trifle more westerly.

I then told him that, with a good wind, I would give the ship eight or nine days to do the run in, and recommended him to let the crew know this, as they must now turn to and arrange, not only how they should leave the ship—in what condition, whether with their clothes and effects, as if they had had time to save them, or quite destitute, as though they had taken to the boats in a hurry—but also make up their minds as to the character of the story they should relate when they got ashore.

He answered that all this was settled, as, of course, I was very well aware; but then my reason for talking to him in this strain was to convince him that I had no suspicion of the diabolical project he was meditating against my life.

You will, perhaps, find it hard to believe that he and the others should be so ignorant of navigation as to be duped by my false reckonings and misstatements of distances. But I can aver from experience that merchant-seamen are, as a rule, as ignorant and thick-headed a body of men as any in this world—and scarcely a handful in every thousand with even a small acquaintance with the theoretical part of their calling. More than a knowledge of practical seamanship is not required from them; and how many are proficient even in this branch? Of every ship's company more than half always seem to be learning their business; furling badly, reefing badly, splicing, scraping, painting, cleaning badly; turning to lazily; slow up aloft, negligent, with an immense capacity of skulking.

I am persuaded that had I not shown Stevens the chart, I could have satisfied him that a southerly course would have fetched the coast of America. The mistake I made was in being too candid and honest with them in the beginning. But then I had no plan formed. I dared not be tricky113 without plausibility, and without some definite end to achieve. Now that I had got a good scheme in my head, I progressed with it rapidly, and I felt so confident of the issue, in the boatswain's pluck and my own energy, that my situation no longer greatly excited my apprehensions, and all that I desired was that the hour might speedily arrive when the boats with their cargo of rascals and cowards should put off and leave the ship.

114

CHAPTER V.

Having no other log-book than my memory to refer to, I pass over six days, in which nothing occurred striking enough for my recollection to retain.

This brought us to Sunday; and on that day at noon we were, as nearly as I can recall, in 37° north latitude and 50° west longitude.

In round numbers Bermuda lies in latitude 32° and longitude 65°. This is close enough for my purpose. We had consequently some distance yet to run before we should heave to off the coast of Florida. But we had for five days carried a strong following wind with us, and were now (heading west115 by south half south) driving eight or nine knots an hour under a fresh wind forward of the port beam.

I own I was very glad to be able to keep well to the norrard of 30°; for had the north-east trade winds got hold of the ship, I should not have been able to accommodate the distances run to my scheme so well as I now could with shifting winds blowing sometimes moderate gales.

The crew continued to behave with moderation. The carpenter, indeed, grew more coarse and offensive in manner as the sense of his importance and of his influence over the men grew upon him; and there were times when Johnson and Fish put themselves rather disagreeably forward; but I must confess I had not looked for so much decency of behaviour as was shown by the rest of the men in a crew who were absolute masters of the vessel.

116 But all the same, I was not to be deceived by their apparent tractableness and quiet exterior. I knew but too well the malignant purpose that underlay this reposeful conduct, and never addressed them but felt that I was accosting murderers, who, when the moment should arrive, would watch their victims miserably drown, with horrid satisfaction at the success of their cruel remedy to remove all chance of their apprehension.

On this Sunday, old Mr. Robertson came on deck for the first time, accompanied by his daughter, who had not before been on the poop in the daytime.

It was my watch on deck; had it been the carpenter's, I should have advised them to keep below.

What I had feared had now come to pass. Mr. Robertson's memory was gone. He could recall nothing; but what was more117 pitiful to see, though it was all for the best so far as he was concerned, he made no effort to recollect. Nothing was suggestive; nothing, that ever I could detect, put his mind in labour. His daughter spoke to me about this melancholy extinction of his memory, but not with any bitterness of sorrow.

"It is better," she said, "that he should not remember the horrors of that shipwreck, nor understand our present dreadful position."

It was indeed the sense of our position that took her mind away from too active a contemplation of her father's intellectual enfeeblement. There was never a more devoted daughter, more tender, gentle, unremitting in her foresight of his wants; and yet, in spite of herself, the feeling of her helplessness would at times overpower her; that strong and beautiful instinct in women118 which makes them turn for safety and comfort to the strength of men whom they can trust, would master her. I knew, I felt through signs touching to me as love, how she looked to me out of her loneliness, out of the deeper loneliness created in her by her father's decay, and wondered that I, a rough sailor, little capable of expressing all the tenderness and concern and strong resolutions that filled my heart, should have the power to inspirit and pacify her most restless moods. In view of the death that might await us—for hope and strive as we might, we could pronounce nothing certain—it was exquisite flattery to me, breeding in me, indeed, thoughts which I hardly noted then, though they were there to make an epoch in my life, to feel her trust, to witness the comfort my presence gave her, to receive her gentle whispers that she had no fear now; that I was her friend; that119 she knew me as though our friendship was of old, old standing!

I say, God bless her for her faith in me! I look back and know that I did my best. She gave me courage, heart, and cunning; and so I owed my life to her, for it was these things that saved it.

She exactly knew the plans concerted by the boatswain and myself, and was eager to help us; but I could find no part for her.

However, this Sunday afternoon, whilst I stood near her, talking in a low voice, her father sitting in a chair that I had brought from the cuddy, full in the sun, whose light seemed to put new life into him—I said to her with a smile—

"If to-night is dark enough, the boatswain must be drowned."

"Yes," she answered, "I know. It will not be too soon, you think?"

120 "No. I shall not be easy until I get him stowed away in the hold."

"You will see," she exclaimed, "that the poor fellow takes plenty to eat and drink with him?"

"A good deal more than he wants is already there," I answered. "For the last three days he has been dropping odds and ends of food down the fore hatch. Let the worst come to the worst, he had smuggled in enough, he tells me, to last him for a fortnight. Besides, the water-casks are there."

"And how will he manage to sleep?"

"Oh, he'll coil up and snug himself away anyhow. Sailors are never pushed for a bedstead: anything and everything serves. The only part of the job that will be rather difficult is the drowning him. I don't know anything that will make a louder splash and sink quickly too, than a box of nails. The121 trouble is to heave it overboard without the man at the wheel seeing me do it; and I must contrive to let him think that the boatswain is aft, before I raise the splash, because if this matter is not ship-shape and carried out cleverly, the man, whoever he may be that takes the wheel, will be set thinking and then get on to talking. Now, not the shadow of a suspicion must attend this."

"May I tell you how I think the man who is steering can be deceived?"

"By all means."

She fixed her eyes on the sea and said—

"I must ask some questions first. When you come on deck, will it be the boatswain's or the carpenter's turn to go downstairs?"

"The carpenter's. He must be turned in before I move."

"And will the same man be at the wheel who steered the ship during the carpenter's watch?"

122 "No. He will be relieved by a man out of the port watch."

"Now I understand. What I think is that the man who comes to take the other one's place at the wheel ought to see the boatswain as he passes along the deck. The boatswain should stand talking with you in full sight of this man, that is, near the wheel, if the night is dark, so that he can hear his voice, if he cannot distinguish his face; and when all is quiet in the fore part of the ship, then you and he should walk away and stand yonder," pointing, as she spoke, to the creak of the poop.

I listened to her with interest and curiosity.

"Some one must then creep up and stand beside you, and the boatswain must instantly slip away and hide himself. The case of nails ought to be ready in one of those boats; you and the person who takes123 the boatswain's place must then go to the boat, and one of you, under pretence of examining her, must get the box of nails out on to the rails ready to be pushed over-boards. Then the new-comer must crouch among the shadows and glide away off the poop, and when he is gone you must push the box over into the sea and cry out."

"The plot is perfect," I exclaimed, struck not more by its ingenuity than the rapidity with which it had been conceived. "There is only one drawback—who will replace the bo'sun? I dare not trust the steward."

"You will trust me?" she said.

I could not help laughing, as I exclaimed, "You do not look like the bo'sun."

"Oh, that is easily done," she replied, slightly blushing, and yet looking at me bravely. "If he will lend me a suit of his clothes, I will put them on."

124 To spare her the slightest feeling of embarrassment, I said—

"Very well, Miss Robertson. It will be a little masquerading, that is all. I will give you a small sou'wester that will hide your hair—though even that precaution should be unnecessary, for if the night is not dark, the adventure must be deferred."

"It is settled!" she exclaimed, with her eyes shining. "Come! I knew I should be able to help. You will arrange with the boatswain, and let me know the hour you fix upon, and what signal you will give me to steal up on deck and place myself near you."

"You are the bravest girl in the world! you are fit to command a ship!" I exclaimed.

She smiled as she answered, "A true sailor's compliment, Mr. Royle." Then with a sudden sigh and a wonderful change125 of expression, making her beauty a sweet and graceful symbol of the ever-changing sea, she cried, looking at her father—

"May God protect us and send us safely home! I dare not think too much. I hope without thinking. Oh, Mr. Royle, how shall you feel when we are starting for dear England? This time will drive me mad to remember!"

126

CHAPTER VI.

I shall never forget the deep anxiety with which I awaited the coming on of the night, my feverish restlessness, the exultation with which I contemplated my scheme, the miserable anguish with which I foreboded its failure.

It was like tossing a coin—the cry involving life or death!

If Stevens detected the stratagem, my life was not worth a rushlight, and the thoughts of Mary Robertson falling a victim to the rage of the crew was more than my mind could be got to bear upon.

Stevens came on deck at four o'clock in the afternoon, and that I might converse with the boatswain without fear of incurring the carpenter's suspicion, I brought a chart from the captain's cabin and spread it on the cuddy table, right under the after skylight, and whilst the boatswain and I hung over it, pretending to be engaged in calculations, we completed our arrangements.

He was struck with the boldness of Miss Robertson's idea, and said he would as soon trust her to take part in the plot as any stout-hearted man. He grinned at the notion of her wearing his clothes, and told me he'd make up a bundle of his Sunday rig, and leave it out for me to put into her cabin.

"She'll know how to shorten what's too lengthy," said he; "and you'd better tell her to take long steps ven she walks, for vimmen's legs travels twice as quick as a man's, and that's how I alvays knows vich sex is hacting before me in the theaytre, though, to be sure, some o' them do dress right up to the hammer, and vould deceive their own mothers."

"Are the hatches off forrard?"

"You leave that to me, Mr. Royle. That'll be all right."

"What weapon have you got?"

"Only a bar of iron the size of my leg," he answered, grimly. "I shouldn't like to drop it on my foot by accident."

We brought our hurried conversation to a close by perceiving the carpenter staring at us stedfastly through the skylight; and whispering that everything now depended upon the night being dark, I repaired with my chart to the cabin I occupied.

I noticed at this time that the lid of one of the lockers stood a trifle open, sustained by the things inside it, which had evidently been tumbled and not put square again.

This, on inspecting the locker, I found to be the case; and remembering that here was the bag of silver I had come across while searching for clothes for old Mr. Robertson, I thrust my hand down to find it. It was gone. "So, Mr. Stevens," thought I, "this is some of your doing, is it? A thief as well as a murderer! You grow accomplished." Well, if he had the silver in his pocket when he quitted the ship, it would only drown him the sooner, should he find himself overboard. There was comfort in that reflection, any way; and I should have been perfectly willing that the silver had been gold, could the rogue's death have been hastened by the transmutation.

A little before six o'clock, at which hour I was to relieve the boatswain in order to take charge of the ship through the second dog-watch, Stevens being in his cabin and all quiet in the after part of the vessel, I went quietly down the ladder that conducted to the steerage, this ladder being situated some dozen feet abaft the mizzen-mast.

All along the starboard side of the ship in this part of her were stowed upwards of seven hundred boxes of tin-tacks, each box about twice the breadth and length of this book in your hand, and weighing pretty heavy. There was nothing else that I could think of that would so well answer the purpose of making a splash alongside, as one of these boxes, and which combined the same weight in so handy and portable a bulk. Anything in wood must float; anything in iron might be missed. All these things had to be carefully considered, for, easy as the job of dropping a weight overboard to counterfeit the sound of a human body fallen into the water may seem, yet in my case the difficulty of accomplishing it[131] successfully, and without the chance of subsequent detection, was immense, and demanded great prudence and foresight.

I conveyed one of these boxes to my cabin, and when four bells were struck (the hands kept the relief bells going for their own sakes, I giving them the time each day at noon), I smuggled it up in a topcoat, and stepped with an easy air on to the poop. The man who had been steering was in the act of surrendering the spokes to another hand, and I took advantage of one of them cutting off a piece of tobacco for the other, which kept them both occupied, to put my coat and the box inside it in the stern sheets of the port quarter-boat, as though it were my coat only which I had deposited there out of the road, handy to slip on should I require it.

The boatswain observed my action without appearing to notice it; and as he passed[132] me on the way to the cuddy, he said that his clothes would be ready by eight bells for the lady, and that I should find them in a bundle near the door.

He would not stay to say more; for I believe that the carpenter had found something suspicious in our hanging together over the chart, and had spoken to this effect to his chums among the men; and it therefore behoved the boatswain and me to keep as clear of each other as possible.

One stroke of fortune, however, I saw was to befall us. The night, unless a very sudden change took place, would be dark.

The sky was thick, with an even and unbroken ground of cloud which had a pinkish tint down in the western horizon, where the sun was declining behind it. The sea was rough, and looked muddy. The wind held steady, but blew very fresh, and had drawn a trifle further to the southwards, so that[133] the vessel was a point off her course. The motion of the ship was very uncomfortable, the pitching sharp and irregular, and she rolled as quickly as a vessel of one hundred tons would.

As the shadows gathered upon the sea, the spectacle of the leaden-coloured sky and waves was indescribably melancholy. Some half-dozen Mother Carey's chickens followed in our wake, and I watched their grey breasts skimming the surface of the waves until they grew indistinguishable on the running foam. The look of the weather was doubtful enough to have justified me in furling the main top-gallant sail and even single reefing the two topsails; but though this canvas did not actually help the ship's progress, as she was close to the wind, and it pressed her over and gave her much leeway, yet I thought it best to let it stand, as it suggested an idea of speed to the men[134] (which I took care the log should confirm), and I should require to make a long reckoning on the chart next day to prove to Stevens that we were fast nearing the coast of Florida.

At eight o'clock I called Stevens, and saw him well upon deck before I ventured to enter the boatswain's berth. I then softly opened the door, and heard the honest fellow snoring like a trooper in his bunk; but the parcel of clothes lay ready, and I at once took them, and knocked lightly on Miss Robertson's door.

She immediately appeared, and I handed her the clothes and also my sou'wester, which I had taken from my cabin after quitting the deck.

"What is to be the signal?" she asked.

"Three blows of my heel over your cabin. There is a spare cabin next door for you to use, as your father ought not to see you."

[135] "I will contrive that he does not see me," she answered. "He fell asleep just now when I was talking to him. I had better not leave him, for if he should wake up and call for me, I should not like to show myself in these clothes for fear of frightening him;

whereas if I stop here I can dress myself by degrees and can answer him without letting him see me."

"There is plenty of time," I said. "The bo'sun relieves the carpenter at midnight. I will join the bo'sun when the carpenter has left the deck. Here is my watch—you have no means of knowing the time without quitting your cabin."

"Is the night dark?"

"Very dark. Nothing could be better. Have no fear," I said, handing her my watch; "we shall get the bo'sun safely stowed below, and with him a crow-bar. The carpenter will find it rather harder136 than he imagines to scuttle the ship. He—I mean the bo'sun—is sound asleep, and snoring like a field-marshal on the eve of glory. His trumpeting is wonderfully consoling, for no man could snore like that who forbodes a dismal ending of life."

I took her hand, receiving as I did so a brave smile from her hopeful, pretty face, and left her.

Without much idea of sleeping, I lay down under a blanket, but fell asleep immediately, and slept as soundly, if not as noisily, as the boatswain, until eleven o'clock.

The vessel's motion was now easier; she did not strain, and was more on an even keel, which either meant that the wind had fallen or that it had drawn aft.

I looked through the porthole, to see if I could make anything of the night, but it was pitch dark. I lighted a pipe to keep137 me awake, and lay down again to think over our plot, and find, if I could, any weakness in it, but felt more than ever satisfied with our plans. The only doubtful point was whether the fellow who went down to scuttle the ship would not get into the forepeak; but if the boatswain could contrive to knock a hole in the bulkhead, he would have the man, whether he got down through the forecastle or the fore-hatch; and this I did not question he would manage, for he was very well acquainted with the ship's hold and the disposition of the cargo.

I found myself laughing once when I thought of the fright the scoundrel (whoever it might be) would receive from the boatswain—he would think he had met the devil or a ghost; but I did not suppose the boatswain would give him much time to be afraid, if he could only bring that crow-bar, as big as his leg, to bear.

138 The sounds of eight bells being struck, set my heart beating rather quickly, and almost immediately I heard Stevens' heavy step coming down the companion-ladder.

I lay quiet, thinking he might look in, as it would better suit my purpose to let him think me asleep. He went and roused out the boatswain, and after a little the boatswain went on deck.

But Stevens did not immediately turn in. I cautiously abstracted the key, and looked through the keyhole, and observed him bring out a bottle of rum and a tumbler from the pantry, and help himself to a stiff glass. He swallowed the fiery draught with his back turned upon the main-deck, that the men, if any were about, should not see him; and drying his lips by running his sleeve, the whole length of his arm, over them, he replaced the bottle and glass, and went to his cabin.

139 This was now my time. There was nothing to fear from his finding me on deck should he take it into his head to come up, since it was reasonable that I, acting as skipper, should at any and all hours be watching the weather, and noting the ship's course, more particularly now, when we were supposed to be drawing near land.

Still, I left my cabin quietly, as I did not want him to hear me, and sneaked up through the companion on tiptoe.

The night was not so pitch dark as I might have expected from the appearance of it through the port-hole; but it was quite dark enough to answer my purpose. For instance, it was as much as I could do to follow the outline of the mainmast, and the man at the wheel and the wheel itself, viewed from a short distance, were lumped into a blotch, though there was a halo of light all around the binnacle.

140 The lamp that was alight in the cuddy hung just abaft the foremost skylight, and I saw that it would be necessary to cover the glass. So I stepped up to the boatswain, who stood near the mizzen-mast.

"Are you all ready, bo'sun?"

"All ready."

"Not afraid of the rats?" I said, with a laugh.

"No, nor wuss than rats," he replied. "Has the lady got my clothes on yet? I should like to see her."

"She'll come when we are ready. That light shining on the skylight must be concealed. I don't want to put the lamp out, and am afraid to draw the curtains for fear the rings should rattle. There's a tarpaulin in the starboard quarter-boat, take and throw it over the skylight whilst I go aft and talk to the fellow steering. Who is he?"

141 "Jim Cornish."

He found the tarpaulin, and concealed the light, whilst I spoke to the man at the wheel about the ship's course, the look of the weather, and so on.

"Now," said I, rejoining the boatswain, "come and take two or three turns along the poop, that Cornish may see us together."

We paced to and fro, stopping every time we reached the wheel to look at the compass.

When we were at the fore end of the poop I halted.

"Walk aft," I said, "and post yourself right in the way of Cornish, that he shan't be able to see along the weather side of the poop."

I followed him until I had come to the part of the deck that was right over Miss Robertson's cabin, and there struck three smart blows with the heel of my boot, at the 142 same time flapping my hands against my breast so as to make Cornish believe that I was warming myself.

I walked to the break of the poop and waited.

In less time than I could count twenty a figure came out of the cuddy and mounted the poop ladder, and stood by my side. Looking close into the face I could see that it was rather too white to be a sailor's, that was all. The figure was a man's, most perfectly so.

"Admirable!" I whispered, grasping her hand.

I posted her close against the screened skylight, that her figure might be on a level with the mizzen-mast viewed from the wheel, and called to the boatswain.

The tone of my voice gave him his cue. He came forward just as a man would to receive an order.

143 "She is here," I said, turning him by the arm to where Miss Robertson stood motionless. "For God's sake get forward at once! Lose no time!"

He went up to her and said—

"I'm sorry I can't see you properly, miss. If this wur daylight I reckon you'd make a handsome sailor, just fit for the gals to go dreamin' an' ravin' about."

With which, and waving his hand, the plucky fellow slipped off the poop like a shadow, and I watched him glide along the main-deck until he vanished.

"Now," whispered I to my companion, "the tragedy begins. We must walk up and down that the man steering may see us. Keep on the left side of the deck; it is higher than where I shall walk, and will make you look taller."

I posted her properly, and we began to measure the deck.

144 Anxious as I was, I could still find time to admire the courage of this girl. At no sacrifice of modesty—no, not even to the awakening of an instant's mirth in me—was her noble and beautiful bravery illustrated. Her pluck was so grand an expression of her English character, that no emotion but that of profound admiration of her moral qualities could have been inspired in the mind of any man who beheld her.

I took care not to go further than the mizzen-rigging, so that Cornish should distinguish nothing but our figures; and after we had paraded the deck awhile I asked her to stand near the quarter-boat in which I had placed the box.

I then got on to the rail and fished out the box smartly, and stood it on the rail.

"Keep your hand upon it," said I, "that it may not roll overboard."

With which I walked right up to Cornish.

145 "Does she steer steady?"

"True as a hair."

"I left my coat this afternoon in one of the quarter-boats. Have you seen it?"

"No."

"Perhaps it's in the starboard-boat."

I pretended to search, and then drawing close to Miss Robertson, said quickly—

"Creep away now. Keep close to the rail and crouch low. Get to your cabin and change your dress. Roll the clothes you are wearing in a bundle and hide them for the present."

She glided away on her little feet, stooping her head to a level with the rail.

All was quiet forward—the main-deck deserted. I waited some seconds, standing with my hand on the box, and then I shoved it right overboard. It fell just as I had expected, with a thumping splash.

Instantly I roared out, "Man overboard!146 Down with your helm! The bo'sun's gone!" and to complete the imposture I bounded aft, cut away a life-buoy, and flung it far into the darkness astern.

Cornish obeyed me literally; put the helm right down, and in a few moments the sails were shaking wildly.

"Steady!" I shouted. "Aft here and man the port main-braces! Bear a hand! the bo'sun's overboard!"

My excitement made my voice resonant as a trumpet, and the men in both watches came scampering along the deck. The shaking of the canvas, the racing of feet, my own and the cries of the crew, produced, as you may credit, a fine uproar. Of course I had foreseen that there would be no danger in bringing the ship aback. The wind though fresh was certainly not strong enough to jeopardize the spars; moreover, the sea had moderated.

147 Up rushed the carpenter in a very short time, rather the worse, I thought, for the dose he had swallowed.

"What's the matter! What the devil is all this?" he bellowed, lurching from side to side as the ship rolled, for we were now broadside on.

"The bo'sun has fallen overboard!" I shouted in his ear; and I had need to shout, for the din of the canvas was deafening.

"Do you say the bo'sun?" he bawled.

"Yes. What shall we do? is it too dark to pick him up?"

"Of course it is!" he cried, hoarse as a raven. "What do you want to do? He's drownded by this time! Who's to find him? Give 'em the proper orders, Mr. Royle!" and he vociferated to the men—"Do you want the masts to carry away? Do you want to be overhauled by the fust wessel as comes this road, and hanged, every148 mother's son of you, because the bo'sun's fallen overboard?"

I stood to leeward gazing at the water and uttering exclamations to show my concern and distress at the loss of the boatswain.

Stevens dragged me by the arm.

"Give 'em the proper orders, I tell ye, Mr. Royle!" he cried. "I say that the bo'sun's drownded, and that no stopping the wessel will save him. Sing out to the men, for the Lord's sake! Let her fill again, or we're damned!"

"Very well," I replied with a great air of reluctance, and I advanced to the poop-rail and delivered the necessary orders. By dint of flattening in the jib-sheets and checking the main-braces, and brailing up the spanker and rousing the foreyards well forward, I got the ship to pay off. The carpenter worked like a madman, bawling149 all the while that if the ship was dismasted all hands would certainly be hanged; and he so animated the men by his cries and entreaties, that more work was done by them in one quarter of an hour than they would have put into treble that time on any other occasion.

It was now one o'clock, so it had not taken us an hour to drown the boatswain, put the ship in irons, and get her clear again.

Stevens came off the main-deck on to the poop, greatly relieved in his mind now that the sails were full and the yards trimmed, and asked me how it happened that the boatswain fell overboard.

I replied, very gravely, that I had come on deck at eight bells, being anxious to see what way the ship was making and how she was heading; that remembering I had left an overcoat in one of the quarter-boats, I150 looked, but could not find it; that I spoke to the boatswain, who told me that he had seen the coat in the stern sheets of the quarter-boat that afternoon, and got on to the poop-rail to search the boat; that I had turned my head for a moment when I heard a groan, which was immediately followed by a loud splash alongside, and I perceived that the boatswain had vanished.

"So," continued I, "I pitched a life-buoy astern and sang out to put the helm down; and I must say, Mr. Stevens, that I think we could have saved the poor fellow had we tried. But you are really the skipper of this ship, and since you objected I did not argue."

"There's no use sayin' we could ha' saved him," rejoined Stevens, gruffly. "I say we couldn't. Who's to see him in the dark? We should have had to burn a flare for the boat to find us, and what with our151 driftin' and their lumpin' about, missing their road, and doing no airthly good, we should ha' ended in losin' the boat."

He did not notice the tarpaulin spread over the skylight, though I had an explanation of its being there had he inquired the meaning of it.

He hung about the deck for a whole hour, though I had offered to take the boatswain's watch, and go turn and turn about with him (Stevens), and he had a long yarn with the man at the wheel, which I contrived to drop in upon after awhile, and found Cornish explaining exactly how the boatswain fell overboard, and corroborating my story in every particular.

Thus laborious as my stratagem had been, it was, as this circumstance alone proved, in no sense too laboured; for had not Cornish seen, with his own eyes, the boatswain and myself standing near the boat152 just before I gave the alarm, he would in all probability have represented the affair in such a way to Stevens as to set him doubting my story, and perhaps putting the men on to search the ship, to see if the boatswain was overboard.

He went below at two o'clock.

The sea fell calm, and the wind shifted round to the nor'ard and westward, and was blowing a steady pleasant breeze at six bells. The stars came out and the horizon cleared, and looking to leeward I beheld at a distance of about four miles the outline of a large ship, which, when I brought the binocular glasses to bear on her, I found under full sail.

She was steering a course seemingly parallel with our own, and as I watched her my brains went to work to conceive in what possible way I could utilize her presence.

At all events, the first thing I had to do153 was to make sail, or she would run away from us; so I at once called up the watch.

Whilst the men were at work the dawn broke, and by the clearer light I perceived that the vessel was making a more westerly course than we, and was drawing closer to us at every foot of water we severally measured. She was a noble-looking merchantman, like a frigate with her painted ports, with double topsail and top-gallant yards, and with skysails set, so that her sails were a wonderful volume and tower of canvas.

The sight of her filled me with emotions I cannot express. As to signalling her, I knew that the moment the men saw me handling the signal-halliards they would crowd aft and ask me what I meant to do. I might indeed hail her if I could sheer the Grosvenor close enough alongside for my voice to carry; but if they failed to hear154 me or refused to help, what would be my position? So surely as I raised my voice to declare our situation, so surely would the crew drag me down and murder me out of hand.

Presently Fish and Johnson came along the main-deck, and while Fish entered the cuddy Johnson came up to me.

"Hadn't you better put the ship about?" he said. "You're running us rather close. The men don't like it."

Seeing that no chance would be given me to make my peril known to the stranger, I formed my resolution rapidly. I called out to the men—

"Johnson wants to 'bout ship. Yonder vessel can see that we are making a free wind, and she'll either think we're mad or that there's something wrong with us if we 'bout ship with a beam wind. Now just tell me what I am to do."

155 "Haul us away from that ship—that's all we want," answered one of them.

At this moment the carpenter came running up the poop ladder, with nothing on but his shirt and a pair of breeches.

"Hallo!" he called out fiercely; "what are you about? Do you want to put us alongside!"

And he bawled out fiercely—"Port your helm! run right away under her stern!"

"If you do that," I exclaimed, very anxious now to show how well-intentioned I was, "you will excite her suspicions. Steady!" I cried, seeing the ship drawing rapidly ahead; "bring her to again a point off her course."

Stevens scowled at me, but did not speak.

The crew clustered up the poop ladder to stare at the ship, and I caught some of them casting such threatening looks at me, that I wanted no better hint of the156 kind of mercy I should receive if I played them any tricks.

"Mr. Stevens," said I, "leave me to manage, and I'll do you no wrong. That ship is making more way than we are, and we shall have her dead on end presently. Then I'll show you what to do."

As I spoke, the vessel which we had brought well on the port-bow hoisted English colours. The old ensign soared gracefully, and stood out at the gaff-end.

"We must answer her," I exclaimed to the carpenter. "You had better bend on the ensign and run it up."

I suppose he knew that there could be no mischievous meaning in the display of this flag, for he obeyed me, though leisurely.

The ship, when she saw that we answered her, hauled her ensign down, and after awhile, during which she sensibly increased157 the distance between us, and had drawn very nearly stern on, hoisted her number.

"Run up the answering pennant," I exclaimed; "it will look civil any way, and it means nothing."

I pointed out the signal to the carpenter, who hoisted it; but I could see by his face that he meant to obey no more orders of this kind.

"Steady as she goes!" cried I, to the fellow steering. "A hand let go the weather mizzen-braces and haul in some of you to leeward."

This manœuvre laid the sails on the mizzen-mast aback; they at once impeded our way, nor, being now right ahead of us, could the people on board the ship see what we had done. The result was the vessel drew away rapidly, I taking care to luff as she got to windward, so as to keep our flying jib-boom in a direct line with her stern.

158 To judge by the way the men glanced at me and spoke to one another, they evidently appreciated this stratagem: and Stevens condescended to say, "That's one for her."

"Better than going about," I answered drily.

"They've hauled down them signals," he said, blinking the point I raised by my remark.

"Yes. She doesn't mean to stop to ask any questions."

The end of this was that in about twenty minutes the ship was three or four miles ahead of us; so not choosing to lose any more time, I swung the mizzen-yards, and got the Grosvenor upon her course again.

Stevens went below to put on his coat and cap and boots in order to relieve me, for it was now four o'clock. The dawn had broken with every promise of a fine day,159 and where the sun rose the sky resembled frost-work, layer upon layer of high delicate clouds, ranged like scale armour, all glittering with silver brightness and whitening the sea, over which they hung with a pale, pearly light.

I was thoroughly exhausted, not so much from the want of rest as from the excitement I had gone through. Still, I had a part to play before I turned in; so I stuck my knuckles in my eyes to rub them open, and waited for Stevens, who presently came on deck, having first stopped on the main-deck to grumble to his crony Fish over his not having had a quarter of an hour's sleep since midnight.

"I'm growed sick o' the sight o' this poop," he growled to me. "Sick o' the sight o' the whole wessel. Fust part o' the woyage I was starved for food. Now, with the skipper overboard, I'm starved for sleep.160 How long are we going to take to reach Florida? Sink me if I shouldn't ha' woted for some nearer coast had I known this woyage wur going to last to the day o' judgment."

"If it don't fall calm," I answered, "I may safely promise to put you off the coast of Florida on Friday afternoon."

He thrust his hands into his breeches' pockets, and stared aft.

"I am very much troubled about the loss of the bo'sun," said I.

"Are you?" he responded, ironically.

"He was a civil man and a good sailor."

"Yes; I dessay he was. But he's no use now."

"He deserved that we should have made an effort to save him."

"Well, you said that before, and I said no; and I suppose I know wot I mean when I says no."

36

161 "But won't the crew think me a heartless rascal for not sending a boat to the poor devil?" I demanded, pretending to lose my temper.

"The bo'sun was none so popular—don't make no mistake; he wasn't one of—— Hell seize me! where are you drivin' to, Mr. Royle? Can't you let a drownded man alone?" he cried, with an outburst of passion. But immediately he softened his voice, and with a look of indescribable cunning, said, "Some of the hands didn't like him, of course; and some did, and they'll be sorry. I am one of them as did, and would ha' saved him if I hadn't feared the masts, and reckoned there'd be no use in the boat gropin' about in the dark for a drownin' man."

"No doubt of that," I replied, in a most open manner. "You know the course, Mr. Stevens? You might set the fore-topmast162 stun'-sail presently, for we shall have a fine day."

And with a civil nod I left him, more than ever satisfied that my stratagem was a complete success.

I bent my ear to Miss Robertson's cabin as I passed, to hear if she were stirring; all was still; so I passed on to my berth, and turned in just as I was, and slept soundly till eight o'clock.

163
CHAPTER VII.

I only saw Miss Robertson for a few minutes at breakfast-time.

The steward as usual carried their breakfast on a tray to the door, and in taking it in she saw me and came forward.

"Is it all well?" she asked, quickly and eagerly.

"All well," I replied.

"He is in the hold," she whispered, "and no one knows?"

"He is in the hold, and the crew believe to a man that he is overboard."

"It is a good beginning," she exclaimed, with a faint smile playing over her pale face.
164 "Thanks to your great courage! You performed your part admirably."

"There is that hateful carpenter watching us through the skylight," she whispered, without raising her eyes. "Tell me one thing before I go—when will the ship reach the part she is to stop at?"

"I shall endeavour to make it Friday afternoon."

"The day after to-morrow!"

She clasped her hands suddenly and exclaimed with a little sob in her voice, "Oh, let us pray that God will be merciful and protect us!"

I had no thoughts for myself as I watched her enter her cabin. The situation was, indeed, a dreadful one for so sweet and helpless a woman to be placed in. I, a rough, sturdy fellow, used to the dangers of the sea, was scared at our position when I contemplated it. Truly might I say that165 our lives hung by a hair, and that whether we were to live or perish dismally would depend upon the courage and promptness with which the boatswain and I should act at the last moment.

It was worse for me that I did not know the exact plans of the mutineers.

I was aware that their intention was to scuttle the ship and leave her, with us on board, to sink. But how they would do this, I did not know. I mean, I could not foresee whether they would scuttle the ship whilst all the crew remained on board, stopping until they knew that the vessel was actually sinking before taking to the boats, or whether they would get into the boat, leaving one man in the hold to scuttle the ship, and lying by to take him off when his work should have been performed.

Either was likely; but one would make 166 our preservation comparatively easy; the other would make it almost impossible.

When I went on deck all hands were at breakfast. The carpenter quitted the poop the moment I showed myself, and I was left alone, none of the crew visible but the steersman.

The breeze was slashing, a splendid sailing wind; the fore-topmast stun'-sail set, every sail round and hard as a drum skin, and the water smooth; the ship bowled along like a yacht in a racing match. Nothing was in sight all round the horizon.

I made sure that the carpenter would go to bed as soon as he had done breakfast; but instead, about twenty minutes after he had left the poop, I saw him walk along the main-deck, and disappear in the forecastle.

After an interval of some ten minutes he reappeared, followed by Johnson, the cook, and a couple of hands. They got upon the 167 port side of the long-boat, and presently I heard the fluttering and screaming of hens.

I crossed the poop to see what was the matter, and found all four men wringing the necks of the poultry. In a short time about sixteen hens, all that remained, lay dead in a heap near the coop. The cook and Johnson gathered them up, and carried them into the galley.

Soon after they returned, and clambered on to the top of the long-boat, the cover of which they pitched off, and fell, each with a knife in his hand, upon the pigs. The noise now was hideous. The pigs squealed like human beings, but both men probably knew their work, for the screeching did not last above five minutes.

The cook, with his face, arms, and breeches all bloody, flung the carcases among the men, who had gathered around 168 to witness the sport, and a deal of ugly play followed. They tossed the slaughtered pigs at each other, and men and pigs fell down with tremendous thuds, and soon there was not a man who did not look as though he had been rolled for an hour in the gutter of a shambles. Their hoarse laughter, their horrible oaths, their rage not more shocking than their mirth, the live men rolling over the dead pigs, their faces and clothes ghastly with blood—all this was a scene which made one abhor oneself for laughing at it, though it was impossible to help laughing sometimes. But occasionally my mirth would be checked by a sudden spasm of terror, when I caught sight of a fellow with an infuriate face, monstrous with its crimson colouring, rush with his knife at another, and be struck down like a ninepin by a dead pig hurled full at his head, before he could deliver his blow.

169 The saturnalia came to an end, and the men cursing, growling, groaning, and laughing—some reeling half stunned, and all panting for breath—surged into the forecastle to clean themselves, while the cook and Johnson carried the pigs into the galley.

I did not quite understand what this scene heralded, but had not long to wait before it was explained.

In twos and threes after much delay, the men emerged and began to wash the decks down. Two got into the long-boat and began to clean her out. Then the carpenter came aft with Johnson, and I heard him swearing at the steward. After a bit, Johnson came forth, rolling a cask of cuddy bread along the deck; after him went the steward, bearing a lime-juice jar, filled of course with rum.

These things were stowed near the foremast. 170 Then all three came aft again (the carpenter superintending the work), and more provisions were taken forward; and when enough was collected, the whole was snugged and covered with a tarpaulin, ready, as I now understood, to be shipped into the long-boat when she should have been swung over the ship's side.

These preparations brought the reality of the position of myself and companions most completely home to me; yet I perfectly preserved my composure, and appeared to take the greatest interest in all that was going forward.

The carpenter came on the poop presently, and went to the starboard quarter-boat and inspected it. He then crossed to the other boat. After which he walked up to me.

"How many hands," he asked, "do you think the long-boat 'ud carry, comfortable?"

171 I measured her with my eye before answering.

"About twenty," I replied.

"One on top o' t'other, like cattle!" he growled. "Why, mate, there wouldn't be standin' room."

"Do you mean to put off from the ship in her?"

"In her and one of them others," he replied, meaning the quarter-boats.

"If you want my opinion, I should say that all hands ought to get into the long-boat. She has heaps of beam, and will carry us all well. Besides, she can sail. It will look better, too, to be found in her, should we be picked up before landing; because you can make out that both quarter-boats were carried away."

"We're all resolved," he answered doggedly. "We mean to put off in the long-boat and one o' them quarter-boats. The172 quarter-boat can tow the long-boat if it's calm. Why I ax'd you how many the long-boat 'ud carry was because we don't want to overload the quarter-boat. We can use her as a tender for stores and water, do you see, so that if we get to a barren place we shan't starve."

"I understand."

"Them two boats 'll be enough, anyways."

"I should say so. They'd carry thirty persons between them," I answered.

To satisfy himself he went and took another look at the boats, and afterwards called Johnson up to him.

They talked together for some time, occasionally glancing at me, and Johnson then went away; but in a few minutes he returned with a mallet and chisel. Both men now got into the port quarter-boat and proceeded, to my rage and mortification, to173 rip a portion of the planking out of her. In this way they knocked several planks away and threw them overboard, and Johnson then got out of her and went to the other boat, and fell to examining her closely to see that all was right; for they evidently had made up their minds to use her, she being the larger of the two.

The carpenter came and stood close to me, watching Johnson. I dare say he expected I would ask him why he had injured the boat; but I hardly dared trust myself to speak to him, so great was my passion and abhorrence of the wretch whose motive in rendering this boat useless was, of course, that we should not be able to save ourselves by her when we found the ship sinking.

When Johnson had done, some men came aft, and they went to work to provision the remaining quarter-boat, passing bags of bread, tins of preserved meat, kegs of174 water, and stores of that description, from hand to hand, until the boat held about a quarter as much again as she was fit to carry.

In the mean time, others were busy in the long-boat, getting her fit for sailing with a spare top-gallant stun'-sail boom and top-gallant stun'-sail, looking to the oars and thole-pins and so forth.

The morning passed rapidly, the crew as busy as bees, smoking to a man, and bandying coarse jokes with one another, and uttering loud laughs as they worked.

The carpenter never once addressed me. He ran about the decks, squirting tobacco-juice everywhere, superintending the work that was going forward, and manifesting great excitement, with not a few displays of bad temper.

A little before noon, when I made ready to take the sun's altitude, the men at work175 about the long-boat suspended their occupation to watch me, and Stevens drew aft, and came snuffling about my heels.

When I sang out eight bells, and went below to work out my observations, he followed me into the cabin, and stood looking on. The ignorance of his distrust was almost ludicrous; I believe he thought I should work out a false reckoning if he were not by, but that his watching would prevent me from making two and two five.

"Now, Mr. Royle," said he, seeing me put down my pencil; "where are we?"

I unrolled the chart upon the table, and drew a line down a rule from the highly imaginary point to which I had brought the ship at noon on the preceding day, to latitude 29°, longitude 74° 30'. "Here is our position at the present moment," I said, pointing to the mark on the chart.

"This here is Floridy, ain't it?" he176 demanded, outlining the coast with his dirty thumb.

"That is Florida."

"Well, I calls it Floridy for short."

"Floridy then. I know what you mean."

"And you give us till the day arter tomorrow to do this bit o' distance in?"

"It doesn't look much on the chart. There's not much room for miles to show in on a square of paper like this."

"Well, we shall be all ready to lower away the boats when you give us the word," said he.

"Perhaps you'll sit down for five minutes, Mr. Stevens, and inform me exactly of your arrangements," I exclaimed; "for it is difficult for me to do my share in this job unless I accurately know what yours is to be."

He looked at me askant, his villainous eyes right in the corners of their sockets;177 but sat down nevertheless, and tilted his cap over his forehead in order to scratch the back of his head.

"I thought you knew what our plans was?" he remarked.

"Why, I've got a kind of general notion of them, but I should like to understand them more clearly."

"Well, I thought they was clear—clear as mud in a wineglass. Leastways, they're clear to all hands."

"For instance, why did you knock a hole in the quarter-boat this morning?"

"I didn't think you'd want that explained," he answered promptly.

"But you see I do, Mr. Stevens."

"Well, we only want two boats, and it 'ud be a silly look-out to leave the third one sound and tight to drift about with the Grosvenor's name writ inside o' her."

"Why?"

178 "Because I says it would."

"How could she drift about if she were up at the davits?"

"How do I know?" he answered morosely. "I'm lookin' at things as may happen. It ain't for me to explain of them."

"Very well," said I, master enough of the ruffian's meaning to require no further information on this point.

"Anything more, Mr. Royle?"

"Yes. The next matter is this: you gave me to understand that we should heave the ship to at night?"

"Sartinly. As soon as ever it comes on dusk, so as we shall have all night before us to get well away."

"Do you mean to leave her with her canvas standing?"

"Just as she is when she's hove to."

"Some ship may sight her, and finding her abandoned, send a crew on board to work her to the nearest port."

I thought this might tempt him to admit that she was to be scuttled, which confession need not necessarily have involved the information that I and the others were to be left on board.

But the fellow was too cunning to hint at such a thing.

"Let them as finds her keep her," he said, getting up. "That's their consarn. Any more questions, Mr. Royle?"

"Are we to take our clothes with us?"

He grinned in the oddest manner.

"No. Them as has wallyables may shove 'em into their pockets; but no kits 'll be allowed in the boats. We're a poor lot o' shipwrecked sailors—marineers as the newspapers calls us—come away from a ship that was settlin' under our legs afore we had the arts to leave her. We jest had time to wittol the boats and stand for the shore. We depend upon Christian kindness for 'elp; and if we falls foul o' a missionary, leave me alone to make him vurship our piety. The skipper he fell mad and jumped overboard. The chief mate he lost his life by springin' into vun o' the boats and missin' of it; and the second mate he manfully stuck to the ship for the love he bore her owners, and we preesume, went down with her."

"Oh!" I exclaimed, forcing a laugh; "then I am not to admit that I am the second mate, when questioned?"

He stared at me as if he were drunk, and cried, "You!" then burst into a laugh, and hit me a slap on the back.

"Ah!" he exclaimed. "I forgot. Of course you'll not be second mate when you get ashore."

"What then?"

"Why, a passenger—a parson—the ship's doctor. We'll tell you wot to say as we go along. Come, get us off this bloomin' coast, will you, as soon as you can," pointing to the chart. "All hands is growin' delikit with care and consarn: as Joe Sampson used to sing—

'Vith care an' consarn
Ve're a vastin' avay.'

And our nerviss systems is that wrought up with fear of our necks, that blowed if we shan't want two months o' strong physicking and prime livin' at the werry least, to make men of us agin arter we're landed."

And with a leering grin and an ugly nod he quitted the cabin.

CHAPTER VIII.

I made up my mind as Stevens left me to bring this terrible time to an end on Friday afternoon, come what might. Let it fall a calm, let it blow a gale, on Friday afternoon I would tell the carpenter that the ship was off the coast of Florida, forty or fifty miles distant.

If, by the boatswain's ruse, I could keep the ship afloat and carry her to Bermuda, it would matter little whether we hove her to one hundred or even two hundred miles distant from the island. The suspense I endured, the horror of our situation, was more than I could bear. I believed that my[183] health and strength would give way if I protracted the ship's journey to the spot where the men would leave her, even for twenty-four hours longer than Friday.

The task before me then was to prepare for the final struggle, to thoroughly mature my plans, to utilize the control I still had over the ship to the utmost advantage, and to put into shape all plausible objections and hints I could think upon, which would be helpful to me if adopted by the crew.

What I most felt was the want of firearms. The revolver I carried was indeed five-chambered, and there was much good fortune in my having been the first to get hold of it. But could I have armed the boatswain or even the steward with another pistol, I should have been much easier in my mind when I contemplated the chances of a struggle between us and the crew.

However, there is no evil that is not[184] attended by some kind of compensation, and I found this out; for taking it into my head that there might be a pistol among Duckling's effects, though I was pretty sure that the weapon he had threatened me with was the one in my possession, I entered his cabin with the intention to begin a search, but had no sooner opened the lid of his chest than I perceived that I had been forestalled, for the clothes were tossed anyway, the pockets turned inside out, and articles taken out of wrappers, as I should judge from the paper coverings that lay among the clothes.

So now I could only hope that Duckling had not had a pistol, since whoever had rifled his box must have met with it. And that Stevens was the thief in this as in the case of the silver I had no doubt at all.

There being now only two of us to keep watch, Stevens and I did not meet at dinner.[185] I took his place whilst he dined, and he then relieved me.

The steward told me they were having a fine feast in the forecastle; that upwards of ten of the fowls which had been strangled in the morning had been put to bake for the men's dinner; that in addition to this they had cooked three legs of pork, and were drinking freely from a jar of rum which the carpenter had ordered him to take forward.

I could pretty well judge that they were enjoying themselves, by the loud choruses they were singing.

Believing they would end in becoming drunk, I knocked on Miss Robertson's door, to tell her on no account to show herself on deck. She gave me her hand the moment she saw me, and gently brought me into the cabin and made me sit down, though I had not meant to stay.

The old gentleman stood with his back to[186] the door, looking through the porthole. Though he heard my voice, he did not turn, and only looked round when his daughter pulled him by the arm.

"How do you do, sir?" he exclaimed, making me a most courtly bow. "I hope you are well? You find us, sir," with a stately wave of the hand, "in wretched accommodation; but all this will be mended presently. The great lesson of life is patience."

And he made me another bow, meanwhile looking hard at me and contracting his brows.

I was more affected by this painful change—this visible and rapid decay, not of his memory only, but of his mind—than I know how to describe. The mournful, helpless look his daughter gave him, the tearless melancholy in her eyes, as she bent them on me, hit me hard.

187 I did not know how to answer him, and could only fix my eyes on the deck.

"This prospect," he continued, pointing to the port-hole, "is exceedingly monotonous. I have been watching it I should say a full half-hour—about that time, my dear, should you not think?—and find no change in it whatever. I witness always the same unbroken line of water, slightly darker, I observe, than the sky which bends to meet it. That unbroken line has a curious effect upon me. It seems to press like a substantial ligature or binding upon my forehead; positively," he exclaimed, with a smile almost as sweet as his child's, "as though I had a cord tied round my head."

He swept his hand over his forehead, as though he could remove the sensation of tightness by the gesture. It was pitiful to witness such a venerable and dignified old 188 gentleman stricken thus in his mind by the sufferings and miserable horrors of shipwreck.

"I think, sir," I said, addressing him with all the respectfulness I could infuse into my voice, "that the uneasiness of which you complain would leave you if you would lie down. The eye gets strained by staring through a port-hole, and that eternal horizon yonder really grows a kind of craze in one's head, if watched too long."

"You are quite right, sir," he replied, making me another bow; and, addressing his daughter, "This gentleman sympathizes with the peculiar inspirations of what I may call monotonous nature."

He looked at her with extraordinary and painful earnestness. Evidently, some recollection had leaped into his mind and quitted him immediately, leaving him bewildered by it.

189 He then said, in a most plaintive voice—

"I will lie down. Your shoulder, my love."

He stretched out his old trembling hand. I got up to help him, but he withdrew from me with an air of offended pride, and reared his figure to its full height.

"This is my daughter, sir," he exclaimed, with cold emphasis; and though I knew he was not accountable for his behaviour, I shrunk back, feeling more completely snubbed than ever I remember being in my life.

With her assistance he got into the bunk, and lay there quite still.

She drew close to me, and obliged me to share the seat she made of the box which had contained the steward's linen.

"You are not angry with him?" she whispered.

"Indeed not."

190 "I shall lose him soon. He will not live long," she said, and tears came into her eyes.

"God will spare him to you, Miss Robertson. Have courage. Our trials are nearly ended. Once ashore he will recover his health—it is this miserable confinement, this gloomy cabin, this absence of the comforts he has been used to, that are telling upon his mind. He will live to recall all this in his English home. The worst has never come until it is passed—that is my creed; because the worst may be transformed into good even when it is on us."

"You have the courage," she answered, "not I. But you give me courage. God knows what I should have done but for you."

I looked into her brave soft eyes, swimming in tears, and could have spoken some 191 deep thoughts to her then, awakened by her words.

I was silent a moment, and then said—

"You must not go on deck to-day. Indeed, I think you had better remain below until I ask you to join me."

"Why? Is there any new danger?"

"Nothing you need fear. The men who fancy themselves very nearly at their journey's end, threaten to grow boisterous. But my importance to them is too great to allow them to offend me yet. Still, it will be best for you to keep out of sight."

"I will do whatever you wish."

"I am sure you will. My wish is to save you—not my wish only—it is my resolution. Trust in me wholly, Miss Robertson. Keep up your courage, for I may want you to help me at the last."

"You must trust in me, too, as my whole trust is in you," she answered, smiling.

192 I smiled back at her, and said—

"Now, let me tell you what may happen—what all my energies are and have been engaged to bring about. On Friday afternoon I shall tell the carpenter that the ship is fifty or sixty miles off the coast of Florida. If the night is calm—and I pray that it may be—the ship will be hove to, that is, rendered stationary on the water; the long-boat will be slung over the side, and the quarter-boat lowered. All this is certain to happen. But now come my doubts. Will the crew remain on board until the man they send into the hold to scuttle the vessel rejoins them? or will they get into the boats and wait for him alongside? If they take to the boats and wait for the man, the ship is ours. If they remain on board, then our preservation will depend upon the bo'sun."

"How?"

193 "He will either kill the man who gets into the hold, or knock him insensible. He will then have to act as though he were the man he has knocked on the head."

"I see."

"If they call to him, he will have to answer them without showing himself. Perhaps he will call to them. They will answer him. They will necessarily muffle their voices that we who are aft may not suspect what they are about. In that case the bo'sun may counterfeit the voice of the man he has knocked on the head successfully."

"But what will he tell them?"

"Why, that his job is nearly finished, and that they had best take to the boats and hold off for him, as he is scuttling her in half a dozen places, and the people aft will find her sinking and make a rush to the boats if they are not kept away. He194 will tell them that when he has done scuttling her, he will run up and jump overboard and swim to them. This, if done cleverly, may decide the men to shove off. We shall see."

"It is a clever scheme," she answered, musingly. "The boatswain's life depends upon his success, and I believe he will succeed in duping them."

"What can be done he will do, I am sure," I said, not choosing to admit that I had not her confidence in the stratagem, because I feared that the more the boatswain should endeavour to disguise his voice the greater would be the risk of its being recognised. "But let me tell you that this is the worst view of the case. It is quite probable that the men will take to the boats and wait for their mate to finish in the hold, not only because it will save time, but because they will imagine it an effectual195 way of compelling us to remain on the vessel.

"What villains! and if they take to the boats?"

"Then I shall want you."

"What can I do?"

"We shall see. There still remains a third chance. The carpenter is, or I have read his character upside down, a born murderer. It is possible that this villain may design to leave the man whom he sends into the hold to sink with the ship. He has not above half a dozen chums, confidential friends, among the crew; and it will be his and their policy to rid themselves of the others as best they can, so as to diminish the number of witnesses against them. If, therefore, they contemplate this, they will leave the ship while they suppose the act of scuttling to be actually proceeding. Now, amongst the many schemes196 which have entered my mind, there was one I should have put into practice had I not feared to commit any action which might in the smallest degree imperil your safety. This scheme was to cautiously sound the minds of the men who were not in the carpenter's intimate confidence; ascertain how far they relished the notion of quitting the ship for a shore that might prove inhospitable, or on which their boats might be wrecked and themselves drowned, and discover by what shrewdness I am master of, how many I might get to come over to my side if the boatswain and myself turned upon Stevens and killed him, shot down Johnson, and fell, armed with my revolver and a couple of belaying pins, upon Cornish and Fish—these three men composing Stevens' cabinet. I say that this was quite practicable, and no very great courage required to execute it, as we should197 have killed or stunned these men before they would be able to resist us."

"There would be nine left."

"Yes; but I should have reckoned upon some of them helping me."

"You could not have depended upon them."

"Well, we have another plan, and I refer to this only to show you a specimen of some of the schemes which have come into my head."

"Mr. Royle, if you had a pistol to give me, I would help you to shoot them! Show me how I can aid you in saving our lives, and I will do your bidding!" she exclaimed, with her eyes on fire.

I put my finger on my lip and smiled.

She blushed scarlet and said, "You do not think me womanly to talk so!"

"You would not hate me were you to know my thoughts," I answered, rising.

198 "Are you going, Mr. Royle?"

"Yes. Stevens, for all I know, may have seen me come in here. I would rather he should find me in my own cabin."

"We see very little of you, considering that we are all three in one small ship," she said, hanging her head.

"I never leave you willingly, and would be with you all day if I might. But a rough sailor like me is poor company."

"Sailors are the best company in the world, Mr. Royle."

"Only one woman in every hundred thinks so—perhaps one in every thousand. Well, you would see less of me than you do if I was not prepared to lay down my life for you. No! I don't say that boastfully. I have sworn in my heart to save you, and it shall cost me my life if I fail. That is what I should have said."

She turned her back suddenly, and I199 hardly knew whether I had not said too much. I stood watching her for a few moments, with my fingers on the handle of the door. Finding she did not move, I went quietly out, but as I closed the door I heard her sob. Now, what had I said to make her cry? I did not like to go in again, and so I repaired to my cabin, wishing, instead of allowing my conversation to drift into a personal current, I had confined it to my plans, which I had not half unfolded to her, but from which I had been as easily diverted as if they were a bit of fiction instead of a living plot that our lives depended on.

During my watch from four to six, Stevens joined me, and asked how "Floridy" would bear from the ship when she was hove to?

I told him that Florida was not an island, but part of the main coast of North200 America, and that he might head the boats any point from N.N.W. to S.S.W. and still, from a distance of fifty or sixty miles, fetch some part of the Florida coast, which I dared say, showed a seaboard ranging four hundred miles long.

This seemed new to him, which more than ever convinced me of his ignorance, for though I had repeatedly pointed out Florida to him, yet he did not know but that it was an island, which might easily be missed by steering the boats a point out of the course given.

He then asked me what compasses we had that we might take with us.

"We shall only want one in the long-boat," I replied; "and there is one on the table in the captain's cabin which will do. Have you got the long-boat all ready?"

"Ay, clean as a new brass farden, and provisioned for a month."

201 "Now let me understand; when the ship is hove to you will sling the long-boat over?"

"I explained all that before," he answered gruffly.

"Not that."

"You're hangin' on a tidy bit about them there boats. What do you think?"

"I suppose my life is as good as yours, and that I have a right to find out how we are to abandon this ship and make the shore," I answered, with some show of warmth, my object being to get all the information from him that was possible to be drawn. "You'll get the long-boat alongside, and all hands will jump into her? Is that it?"

"Why, wot do you think we'd get the boat alongside for if we didn't get into her?" he replied, with a kind of growling laugh.

202 "Will anybody be left on the ship?"

"Anybody left on the ship?" he exclaimed, fetching a sudden breath: "Wot's put that in yer head?"

"I was afraid that that yellow devil, the cook, might induce you to leave the steward behind to take his chance to sink or swim in her, just out of revenge for calling bad pork good," said I, fixing my eyes upon him.

"No, no, nothen of the sort," he replied quickly, and with evident alarm. "Curse the cook! d'ye think I's skipper to give them kind o' orders?"

"Now you see what I am driving at," I said, laying my hand on his arm, and addressing him with a smile. "I really did think you meant to leave the poor devil of a steward behind. And what I wanted to understand was how you proposed to manage with the boats to prevent him boarding you—that is why I was curious."

203 The suspicious ruffian took the bait as I meant he should; and putting on an unconcerned manner, which fitted him as ill as the pilot jacket which he had stolen from the captain he had murdered, and which he was now wearing, inquired, "What I meant by that? If they left the steward behind—not that they was goin' to, but to say it, for the sake o' argyment—what would the management of the boats have to do with preventin' him boardin' of them? He didn't understand."

"Oh, nothing," I replied with a shrug. "Since we are to take the steward with us, there's an end of the matter."

"Can't you explain, sir?" he cried, striving to suppress his temper.

"It is not worth the trouble," said I; "because, don't you see, if even you had made up your mind to leave the steward on the ship, you'd only have one man to deal204 with. What put this matter into my head was a yarn I read some time ago about a ship's company wishing to leave their vessel. There were only two boats which were serviceable, and these wouldn't hold above two-thirds of the crew. So the men conspired among themselves—do you understand me?"

"Yes, yes, I'm a-followin' of you."

"That is, twelve men out of a crew composed of eighteen hands resolved to lower the boats and get away, and leave the others to shift for themselves. But they had to act cautiously, because, don't you see, the fellows who were to be left behind would become desperate with the fear of death, and if any of them contrived to get into the boats, they might begin a fight, which, if it didn't capsize the boats, was pretty sure to end in a drowning match. Of course, in our case, as I have said, even supposing you had 205 made up your mind to leave the steward behind, we should have nothing to fear, because he would be only one man. But when you come to two or three, or four men driven mad by terror, then look out if they get among you in a boat; for fear will make two as strong as six, and I shouldn't like to be in the boat where such a fight was taking place."

"Well, but how did them other chaps manage as you're tellin' about?"

"Why, they all got into the boats in a lump, and shoved off well clear of the ship. The others jumped into the water after them, but never reached the boats. But all this doesn't hit our case. You wished me to explain, and now you know my reasons for asking you how you meant to manage with the boats. Do not forget that there is a woman among us, and a fight at the last moment, when our lives may depend 206 upon orderliness and coolness, may drown us all."

And so saying I left him, under pretence of looking at the compass.
207
CHAPTER IX.

I had no reason to suppose that the hints I took care to wrap up in my conversation with Stevens would shape his actions to the form I wished them to take; but though they did no good, they would certainly do me no harm, and it was at least certain that my opinion was respected, so that I might hope that some weight would attach to whatever suggestions I offered.

Nothing now remained to be done but to wait the result of events; but no language can express an idea of my anxiety as the hours passed, bringing us momentarily closer to the dreaded and yet wished-for issue.

208 Some of the men got intoxicated that afternoon, and I believe two of them had a desperate set to; they sang until they were tired, and for tea had more hot roast pork and fowls.

But the majority had their senses, and kept those who were drunk under; so that the riot was all forward.

I wondered what the boatswain would think of the shindy over his head, and whether he had a watch to tell the time by. His abode was surely a very dismal one, among the coals in the forepeak, and dark as night, with plenty of rats to squeak about his ears, and the endless creaking and complaining of the timbers under water.

A terrible idea possessed me once. It was that he might be asleep when the man went down to scuttle the ship, who, of course, would take a candle with him, and find him lying there.

209 But there was no use in imagining evil. I could only do what was possible. If we were doomed to die, why, we must meet our fate heroically. What more?

It blew freshly at eleven o'clock, and held all night. I kept all the sail on the ship that she would bear, and up to noon next day we spanked along at a great pace.

Then the wind fell light and veered round to the north; but this did not matter to me, for I showed the carpenter a run on the chart which convincingly proved to him that, even if we did no more than four knots an hour until next day, we should be near enough to the coast of Florida to heave to.

This afternoon the men made preparations to swing the long-boat over the side, clapping on strops to the collar of the mainstay, and forward round the tressel-tree, ready to hook on the tackles to lift the 210 boat out of her chocks. Their eagerness to get away from the ship was well illustrated by these early preparations.

All that day they fared sumptuously on roast pork, and whatever took their fancy among the cuddy stores, but drank little, or at all events not enough to affect them, though there was sufficient rum in the hold to kill them all off in a day, had they had a mind to broach the casks.

Towards evening we sighted no less than five ships, two standing to the south and the others steering north. The spectacle of these vessels fully persuaded Stevens that we were nearing the coast, he telling me he had no doubt they were from the West Indies, which he supposed were not more than four hundred miles distant.

I did not undeceive him.

I saw Miss Robertson for a few minutes 211 that evening to repeat my caution to her not to show herself on deck.

The men were again at their pranks in the forecastle, sky-larking as they call it at sea, and, though not drunk, they were making a tremendous noise. One of them had got a concertina, and sat playing it, tailor-fashion, on top of the capstan, and some were dancing, two having dressed themselves up as women in canvas bonnets, and blankets round them to resemble skirts.

Fun of this sort would have been innocent enough had there been any recognized discipline to overlook it; but from decent mirth to boisterous, coarse disorder, is an easy step to sailors, and in the present temper of the crew the least provocation might convert the ship into a theatre for exhibitions of horse-play which, begun in vanity, might end in criminal excesses.

212 During my brief conversation with Miss Robertson, I asked her an odd question—Could she steer a ship?

She answered, "Yes."

"You say 'yes' because you will try if you are wanted to do so," I said.

"I say 'yes' because I really understand how to use the wheel," she replied, seriously.

"Where did you learn?"

"During our voyage to the Cape of Good Hope. I used to watch the man steering, and observe him move the wheel so as to keep the compass card steady. I told Captain Jenkinson I should like to learn to steer, and he would often let me hold the wheel, and for fun give me orders."

"Which way would you pull the spokes if I told you to put the helm to starboard?"

"To the left," she answered, promptly.

"And if I said 'hard over?'"

213 "If the wind was blowing on the left hand side I would push the wheel to the right until I could push it no further. You can't puzzle me, indeed. I know all the steering terms. Really, I can steer."

I quite believed her, though I should never have dreamt of her proficiency in this matter, and told her that if we succeeded in getting away from the boats, she would be of the utmost importance to us, because then there would be three men to work the ship, whereas two only would be at liberty if one had to take the wheel.

*****

And now I come to Friday.

We were keeping no regular watches. Stevens, ever distrustful of me, was markedly so now that our voyage was nearly ended. He was incessantly up and down, looking at the compass, computing the ship's speed by staring at the passing214 water, and often engaged, sometimes on the poop, sometimes on the forecastle, in conversation with Fish, Cornish, Johnson, and others.

He made no inquiries after Mr. or Miss Robertson; he appeared to have forgotten their existence. I also noticed that he shirked me as often as he could, leaving the deck when I appeared, and mounting the ladder the furthest from where I stood when he came aft from the main-deck.

The dawn had broken with a promise of a beautiful day; though the glass, which had been dropping very slowly all through the night, stood low at eight o'clock that morning. The sun, even at that early hour, was intensely hot, and here and there the pitch in the seams of the deck adhered to the soles of one's boots, while the smell of the paint-work rose hot in the nostrils.

There was a long swell, the undulations215 moderate though wide apart, coming from the westward; the clouds were very high, and the sky a dazzling blue, and the wind about north, very soft and refreshing.

The men were quiet, and continued so throughout the day. Many of them, as well as the carpenter, incessantly gazed around the horizon, evidently fearing the approach of a vessel; and some would steal aft and look at the compass, and then go away again.

We were under all plain sail, and the ship, as near as I could tell, was making about five knots an hour, though the log gave us seven, and I logged it seven on the slate in case of any arguments arising.

When I came on deck with my sextant in hand to take sights, I was struck by the intent expressions on the faces of the crew, the whole of whom, even including the cook, had collected on the poop, or stood upon the ladders waiting for me.

216 When I saw them thus congregated, my heart for a moment failed me.

The tremendous doubt crossed my mind—were they acquainted with the ship's whereabouts? Did they know, had they known all through, that I was deceiving them?

No!

As I looked at them I became reassured. Theirs was an anxiety I should have been blind to misconstrue. The true expression on their faces represented nothing but eager curiosity to know whether our journey were really ended, or whether more time must elapse before they could quit the ship which they had rendered accursed with the crime of murder, and which as I well knew, from what Stevens had over and over again let fall, they abhorred with all the terrors of vulgar conscience.

Having made my observations, I was217 about to quit the poop, when one of the men called out—

"Tell us what you make it."

"I will when I have worked it out," I replied.

"Work it out here, whilst we looks on."

"Do any of you understand navigation?"

There was no reply.

"Unless you can count," said I, "you'll not be able to follow me."

"Two and two and one makes nine," said a voice.

"What do ye mean by jokin'? You ought to be ashamed o' yourself," exclaimed one of the men. And then there was a blow, and immediately after an oath.

"If you want me to work out these sights in your presence, I'll do so," said I.

And I went below to get the things I required, leaving my sextant on deck to show them that I meant to be honest.

218 When I returned, they were all around the skylight, gazing at the sextant as though it were an animal; no man taking the liberty to touch it, however.

They came, hustling each other about me as I sat on the skylight working out my figures, and I promise you their proximity, coupled with my notion that they might suspect I had been deceiving them, did not sharpen my wits so as to expedite my calculations.

I carried two reckonings in my head—false, and the true; and finding our actual whereabouts to be ninety-eight miles from Bermuda, the islands bearing W.S.W. as straight as a line, I unfolded the chart, and giving them the imaginary longitude and latitude, put my finger upon the spot we were supposed to have reached, exclaiming,

"Now you can see where we are!"

"Just make a small mark there with 219 your pencil, will you?" said Johnson; "then all hands can have a look."

I did so, and quitted the skylight, surrendering the chart to the men, who made a strange picture as they stood poring over it, pointing with their brown forefingers and arguing.

"There's no question I can answer, is there?" said I to the carpenter.

"Mates, is there anything you want to say to Mr. Royle?" he exclaimed.

"When are we going to heave the ship to?" asked Fish.

"That's for you to answer," I rejoined.

"Well, I'm not for standin' too close in shore," said Fish.

"How fur off do you say is this here Florida coast?" asked Johnson.

"About sixty miles. Look at the chart."

"And every minute brings us nearer," said a man.

220 "That's true," I replied. "But you don't want to leave the ship before dusk, do you?"

The men looked at each other as though they were not sure that they ought to confide so much to me as an answer to my question would involve. I particularly took notice of this, and felt how thoroughly I was put aside by them in their intentions.

The carpenter said, "You'll understand our arrangements by-and-by, Mr. Royle. How's the wind?"

"About north," said I.

"Mates, shall we bring the yards to the masts and keep the leeches liftin' till we're ready to stop her?"

"The best thing as can happen," said Johnson.

"She'll lie to the west'ards at that, and 'll look to be sailin' properly if a vessel sights her; and she'll make no way neither," said Stevens.

221 "You can't do better," I exclaimed.

So the helm was put down, and as the men went to work I descended to my cabin.

The steward's head was at the pantry door, and I called to him, "Bring me a biscuit and the sherry."

I wanted neither, but I had something to say to him; and if Stevens saw him come to my cabin with a tray in his hand he was not likely to follow and listen at the door.

The steward put the tray down and was going away, when I took him by the arm and led him to the extremity of the cabin.

"Do you value your life?" I said to him in a whisper.

He stared at me and turned pale.

"Just listen," I continued. "At dusk this evening the men are going to leave the ship in the boats. They are going to scuttle the ship first that she may fill222 with water and sink. It is not their intention to take us with them."

"My God!" he muttered, trembling like a freezing man: "are we to be left on board to sink?"

"That is what they mean. But the bo'sun, whom they believe to be drowned, is in the hold ready to kill the man who goes down to scuttle the ship. If we act promptly we may save our lives and get away from the ruffians. There are only three of us, but we must fight as though we were twelve men if it should come to our having to fight. Understand that. When once the men are in the boats no creature among them must ever get on board again alive. Hit hard—spare nothing! If we are beaten, we are dead men; if we conquer, our lives are our own."

"I'll do my best," answered the steward, the expression on whose face, however, was223 anything but heroical. "But you must tell me what to do, sir. I shan't know, sir. I never was in a fight, and the sight of blood is terrifying to me, sir."

"You'll have to bottle up your fears. Don't misunderstand me, steward. Every man left on board this ship to drown will look to his companions to help him to save his life. And by all that's holy, if you show any cowardice, if you skulk, if you do not fight like forty men, if you do not stick by my side and obey my words like a flash of lightning, as sure as you breathe I'll put a bullet through your head. I'll kill you for not helping me."

And I pulled out the pistol from my pocket and flourished it under his nose.

He recoiled from the weapon with his eyes half out of his head, and gasped—

"What am I to use, sir?"

"The first iron belaying-pin you can224 snatch up," I answered. "There are plenty to be found. And now be off. Not a look, not a word! Go to your work as usual. If you open your mouth you are a dead man."

He went away as pale as a ghost. However, cur as he was, I did not despair of his turning to at the last moment. Cowards will sometimes make terrible antagonists. The madness of fear renders them desperate, and in their frenzy they will do more execution than the brave deliberate man.

I did not remain long off the poop, being too anxious to observe the movements of the crew.

I found the breeze slackening fast, with every appearance of a calm in the hot, misty blue sky, and the glassy aspect of the horizon. The lower sails flapped to every motion of the ship, and lying close225 to what little wind there was, we made no progress at all.

The promise of a calm, though favourable to the intentions of the men, in so far as it would keep the horizon clear of sailing ships, and so limit the probability of their operations being witnessed to the chance of a steamer passing, was a blow to me; as one essential part of my scheme, that of swinging the mainyards round, and getting way on the ship, when the men had left her, would be impracticable.

The glass, indeed, stood low, but then this might betoken the coming of more wind than I should want, a gale that would detain the men on the ship, and force them to defer the scheme of abandoning her for an indefinite period.

They had gone to dinner, but were so quiet that the vessel seemed deserted, and nothing was audible but the clank of the226 tiller-chains and the rattling of the sails against the masts.

Stevens was forward, apparently having his dinner with the men. In glancing through the skylight, I saw Mary Robertson looking up at me. I leaned forward, so that my face was concealed from the man at the wheel—the only person on deck besides myself—and whispered—

"Keep up your courage, and be ready to act as I may direct."

"I am quite ready," she answered.

"Remain in your cabin," I said, "and don't let the men see you;" for it had flashed upon me that if the crew saw her they might force her to go along with them in the boats.

"I wanted a little brandy for papa," she answered. "He is very poorly and weak, and rambles terribly in his talk."

She turned to hide her tears from me, and prevent me witnessing her struggles to restrain them. She would feel their impotence, the mockery of them at such a time; besides, dear heart, she would think I should distrust her courage if she let me see her weep.

The steward came forward under the skylight as she entered her cabin, and said—

"I will fight for my life, sir."

"That is my advice to you."

"I will do my best. I have been thinking of my wife and child, sir."

"Hush!" I cried. "Not so loud. If your courage fails you, there is a girl in that cabin there, who will show you how to be brave. Remember two things—act quickly and strike hard; and for God's sake don't fall to drinking to pull up your nerves. If I find you drunk I will call upon the men to drown you."

And with this injunction I left the skylight.

The men remained a great while in the forecastle, all so quiet that I wondered whether some among them were even now below scuttling the ship. But they would hardly act so prematurely. To be sure, it would take a long time for the ship to fill, bored even in half a dozen places by an auger; but until the evening fell, and they were actually in the boats, they could not be sure that a wind would not spring up to oblige them to keep to the ship.

I remained on deck, never thinking of dinner, watching the weather anxiously.

An ordinary seaman came aft to relieve the wheel; but finding that the ship had no steerage way on her, he squatted himself on the taffrail, pulled out a pipe and began to smoke. I took no notice of him.

Shortly afterwards Stevens came along the main-deck and mounted the poop.

"A dead calm," said he, after sweeping the horizon with his hand over his eyes, "and blessedly hot."

"Is the ship to be left all standing?" I inquired.

"What do you think?" he replied, with an air of indifference, casting his eyes aloft.

"I should snug her, certainly."

"Why?" he demanded, folding his arms, and staring at me as he leaned against the poop-rail.

"Because, should she drift, and be overhauled by another ship, it will look more ship-shape if she is found snug, as though she had been abandoned in a storm."

"There's something in that," he answered, without shifting his position.

"Shall I tell the men to shorten sail?"

"If you like," he replied, grinning in my face.

I pretended not to observe his odd manner, being very anxious to get in all the sail that I could whilst there were men to do it. So I sang out, "All hands shorten sail!"

The men on the forecastle stared, and burst into a laugh; and one of a group on the main-deck, who were inspecting the provisions for the long-boat, which lay under a tarpaulin, exclaimed—

"Wot's goin' to happen?"

I glanced at the carpenter, who still surveyed me with a broad grin, and walked aft. I was a fool not to have anticipated this. What was it to the crew whether the ship sank with all sails standing or with all sails furled?

I was too restless to go below; but to dissemble my terrible anxiety as well as I could, I lighted a pipe and crouched in the shadow of the mizzen-mast out of the way of the broiling sun.

The breeze had utterly gone. The sea231 was glassy, and white and long wreaths of mist stood, down in the south, upon the horizon. As I looked at the ship, at her graceful spaces of canvas lowering upon the fine and delicate masts, her white decks, her gleaming brass-work, the significance of the crime meditated by the crew was shocking to me. The awful cold-bloodedness with which they meant to sink the beautiful vessel, with the few poor lives who were to be left defenceless on board, overwhelmed me with horror and detestation. So atrocious an act I thought the Almighty would not surely permit. Could not I count upon His mercy and protection? Remembering that I had not sought Him yet, I pulled off my cap, and without kneeling—for I durst not kneel with the eyes of the men upon me—I mutely invoked His heavenly protection. I pleaded with all the strength of my heart for the sweet and helpless girl232 whom, under His divine providence, I had already rescued from one dreadful fate, and whom, under His sure guidance, I might yet preserve from the slow and bitter death which the crew had planned that we should suffer.

It was not until six o'clock that the carpenter ordered the men to get the long-boat over. But just before he called out I had noticed, with a leap of joy in me, that the water out in the north-west was dark as with the shadow of a cloud upon it.

Though this was no more than a cat's paw, and travelled very slowly, I was certain, not only from the indications of the barometer, but from the complexion of the sky, that wind was behind.

The men did not appear to notice it, and when the carpenter sang out the order all hands went to work briskly.

Some ran aloft with tackles, which they233 made fast to the starboard fore and main yard-arms; others hooked on tackles to the straps which were already round the tressel-tree and collar of the mainstay. But willingly as they worked, even these preliminary measures ran into a great deal of time, and before they had done, a light breeze had come down on the ship and taken her aback.

The carpenter, seeing this, clapped some hands on to the fore and mizzen braces, and filled the fore and after sails. The ship was therefore hove to with her head at west.

This done, he went to the wheel, put the helm amidship and made it fast; and then went forward again to superintend the work.

I took up my position on the starboard side of the poop, close against the ladder, and there I remained. I scanned the faces of the men carefully, and found all hands234 present, including the cook. I thus knew that no man was below in the hold, and it was now my business to watch closely that I might miss the man who should have the job to scuttle the ship.

The breeze died away, but in the same direction whence it had come was another shadow, more defined and extending far to the north.

The men had begun their work late, and as they knew that they had little or no twilight to count upon, laboured hard at the difficult task of raising the long-boat out of her chucks and swinging her clear of the bulwarks.

It was close upon seven o'clock before they were ready to hoist. They took the end of one fall to the capstan on the main-deck, the other they led forward through a block, and presently up rose the boat until it was on a level with the bulwarks. Then 235 the yard-arm tackles were manned, the midship falls slacked off, and the big boat sank gently down into the water.

She was brought alongside at once, and three men jumped into her. Then began the process of storing the provisions. This was carried on by five men, while the remaining three came aft, and whilst one got into the quarter-boat, the other two lowered her.

At this moment I missed the carpenter.

I held my breath, looking into the boats and all round.

He was not to be seen.

I strained my ear at the foremost skylight, conceiving that he might have entered the cuddy.

All was silent there.

Beyond the shadow of a doubt, he it was who had planned the scuttling of the ship, and he it was who had left the deck to do it.

236 It was a supreme moment. I had not contemplated that he would be the man who should bore the hole. If the boatswain killed him——!

Great God! the hands were on deck—all about us! If he did not return, they would seek him. He was their leader, and they were not likely to quit the ship without him.

The hair stirred on my head; the sweat stood in beads on my face. I bit my lip half through to control my features, and stood waiting for—I knew not what!

237

CHAPTER X.

The men went on busily provisioning the long-boat, some whistling gay tunes, others laughing and passing jokes, all in good spirits, as though they were going on a holiday expedition.

The shadow on the horizon was broadening fast, and the sun was sinking quickly, making the ocean blood-red with its burning effulgence, and veining the well-greased masts with lines of fire.

What had happened?

Even now, as I thought, was the villain lying dead, with the auger in his hand?

The minutes rolling past seemed eternal. 238 Five, ten, twenty minutes came and went. The sun's lower limb was close against the water-line, sipping the ruby splendour it had kindled. The breeze was now close at hand, but we still lay in a breathless calm, and the sails flapped softly to the tuneful motion of the deep.

Then some of the men who remained on deck went over the ship's side, leaving four of the crew on the main-deck close against the gangway. These men sometimes looked at me, sometimes into the cuddy, sometimes forward, but none of them spoke.

Now the sun was half hidden, and the soft breeze blowing upon the sails, outlined the masts against those which were backed.

Suddenly—and I started as though I had beheld a ghost—the carpenter came round from before the galley, and walked quickly to the gangway.

239 "Over with you, lads!" he cried.

Like rats leaping from a sinking hull they dropped, one after the other, into the long-boat, the carpenter going last. Their painter was fast to a chain-plate, and they cast it adrift. The quarter-boat was in tow, and in a few minutes both boats stood at some two or three cables' lengths from the ship, the men watching her.

The last glorious fragment of the sinking sun fled, and darkness came creeping swiftly over the sea.

I had stood like one in whom life had suddenly been extinguished—too much amazed to act. Seeing the carpenter return, I had made sure that he had killed the boatswain; but his behaviour contradicted this supposition. Had he been attacked by the boatswain and killed him, would he have quitted the ship without revenging himself upon me, whom he would240 know to be at the bottom of this conspiracy against his life?

What, then, was the meaning of his return, his collected manner, his silent exit from the ship? Had the boatswain, lying hidden, died? The thought fired my blood. Yes, I believed that he had died—that the carpenter had performed his task unmolested without perceiving the corpse—and that, whilst I stood there, the water was rushing into the ship's hold!

I flung myself off the poop, and bounded forward. In the briefest possible time I was peering down the forescuttle.

"Below there!" I called.

There was no answer.

"Below there, I say, boatswain!"

My cry was succeeded by a hollow, thumping sound.

"Below there!" I shouted, for the third time.

241 I heard the sounds of a foot treading on something that crunched under the tread.

"I am Mr. Royle. Bo'sun, are you below? For God Almighty's sake answer and let me know that you are living."

"Have the skunks cleared out?" responded a voice, and, stumbling as he moved, the boatswain came under the forescuttle and turned up his face.

"What have you done?" I cried, almost delirious.

"Why, plugged up two on 'em. There's only one more," he answered.

"One more what?"

"Leaks—holes—whatever you call 'em."

So saying, he shouldered his way back into the gloom.

It was now all as clear as daylight to me. I waited some minutes, bursting with impatience and anxiety, during which242 I heard him hammering away like a caulker. My fear was that the men would discover that they had omitted to put a compass in the boats, and that they would return for one. There were other things, too, of which they might perceive the omission, and row to the ship to obtain them before she sank.

Just as I was about to cry out to him to bear a hand, the boatswain's face gleamed under the hatchway.

"Have you done?" I exclaimed.

"Ay, ay."

"Is she tight?"

"Tight as a cocoa-nut."

"Up with you, then! There is a bit of a breeze blowing. Let us swing the mainyards and get way upon the ship. They are waiting to see her settle before they up sail. It is dark enough to act. Hurrah, now!"

243 He came up through the forecastle and followed me on to the main-deck.

Though not yet dark, the shadow of the evening made it difficult to distinguish faces even a short distance off. There was a pretty little wind up aloft rounding the royals and top-gallant sails, and flattening the sails on the mainyards well against the masts.

I stopped a second to look over the bulwarks, and found that the boats still remained at about three cable-lengths from the ship. They had slipped the mast in the long-boat; but I noticed that the two boats lay side by side, four men in the quarter-boat, and the rest in the long-boat, and that they were handing out some of the stores which had been stowed in the quarter-boat, to lighten her.

"We must lose no time, Mr. Royle," exclaimed the boatswain. "How many hands can we muster?"

244 "Three."

"That'll do. We can swing the mainyard. Who's the third?—the steward? Let's have him out."

I ran to the cuddy and called the steward. He came out of the pantry.

"On to the poop with you!" I cried. "Right aft you'll find the bo'sun there. Miss Robertson!"

At the sound of her name she stepped forth from her cabin.

"The men are out of the ship," I exclaimed. "We are ready to get way upon her. Will you take the wheel at once?"

She was running on to the poop before the request was well out of my mouth.

The boatswain had already let go the starboard main-braces; and as I rushed aft he and the steward were hauling to leeward. I threw the whole weight of my 245 body on the brace, and pulled with the strength of two men.

"Put the wheel to starboard!" I called out; and the girl, having cast off the lashing with marvellous quickness, ran the spokes over.

"By God, she's a wonder!" cried the boatswain, looking at her.

And so was he. The muscles on his bare arms stood up like lumps of iron under the flesh as he strained the heavy brace.

The great yards swung easily; the topsail, top-gallant, and royal yards came round with the mainyard, and swung themselves when the sails filled.

There was no time to gather in the slack of the lee-braces. I ran to windward, belayed the braces, and raised a loud cry.

"They're after us, bo'sun!—they're after us!"

We might have been sure of that; for 246 if we had not been able to see them we could have heard them: the grinding of the oars in the rowlocks, the frothing of the water at the boat's bows, the cries and oaths of the men in the long-boat, inciting the others to overtake us.

Only the quarter-boat was in pursuit as yet; but in the long-boat they were rigging up the stun'-sail they had shipped, meaning, as they were to windward, to bear down upon us.

There was no doubt that they guessed their scheme had been baffled by discerning three men on deck. The carpenter at least knew that old Mr. Robertson was too ill to leave his cabin, and failing him he would instantly perceive that a trick had been played; and though he could not tell in that light and at that distance who the third man was, he would certainly know that this third man's presence on board 247 implied the existence of a plot to save the ship.

As the boat approached I perceived that she was rowed by four men and steered by a fifth, and presently, hearing his voice, I understood that this man steering was Stevens.

The ship had just got way enough upon her to answer her helm. Already we were drawing the long-boat away from our beam on to the quarter.

I shouted to Miss Robertson "Steady! keep her straight as she is!" for even now we had brought the wind too far aft for the trim of the yards.

"Steward," I cried, "whip out one of those iron belaying-pins, and stand by to hammer away."

We then posted ourselves, the boatswain and the steward at the gangway, and I half-way up the poop ladder, each with a heavy belaying-pin in his hand, ready to receive the scoundrels who were making for the starboard main-chains.

The boat, urged furiously through the water, came up to us hand over fist, the carpenter cursing us furiously, and swearing that he would do for us yet.

I got my pistol ready, meaning to shoot the ruffian the moment he should be within reach of the weapon, but abandoned this intention from a motive of hate and revenge. I knew if I killed him as he sat there in the stern sheets, that the others would take fright and run away; and such was my passion, and the sense of our superiority over them from our position in the ship as against theirs in the boat, that I made up my mind to let them come alongside and get into the chains, so that we might kill them all as a warning to the occupants of the long-boat, who were now coming down upon us before the breeze.

I took one glance at Miss Robertson: her figure was visible by the side of the wheel. She was steering as steadily as any sailor, and, with an emotion of gratitude to God for giving us such help, and her so much courage at this supreme moment, I addressed all my energies to the bloody work before me.

The boat dashed alongside, and the men threw in their oars. The fellow in the bow grabbed hold of one of the chain-plates, passed the boat's painter around it, hauled it short and made it fast with incredible activity and speed. Then pulling their knives out of the sheaths they all came clambering into the main-chains.

So close as they now were, I could make out the faces of the men. One was big Johnson, another Cornish, the third Fish, the fourth, Schmidten.

I alone was visible. The boatswain and the steward stood with uplifted arms ready to strike at the first head that showed itself.

The carpenter sprang on to the bulwark just where I stood. He poised his knife to stab me under the throat.

"Now, you murderous treacherous ruffian!" I cried at the top of my voice, "say your prayers!"

I levelled the pistol at his head, the muzzle not being a yard away from his face, and pulled the trigger. The bright flash illuminated him like a ray of lightning. He uttered a scream shrill as a child's, but terrific in intensity, clapped his hands to his face, and fell like a stone into the main-chains.

"It is your turn now!" I roared to Johnson, and let fly at him. He was holding on to one of the main shrouds in the act of springing on to the deck. I missed his head, but struck him in the arm, I think; for he let go the shroud with a deep groan, reeled backwards, and toppled overboard, and I heard the heavy splash of his body as he fell.

But we were not even now three to three, but three to one; for the boatswain had let drive with his frightful belaying-pin at Fish's head, just as that enormous protuberance had shown itself over the bulwark, and the wretch lay dead or stunned in the boat alongside; whilst the steward, who had secreted a huge carving-knife in his bosom, had stabbed the Dutchman right in the stomach, leaving the knife in him; and the miserable creature hung over the bulwark, head and arms hanging down towards the water, and suddenly writhing as he thus hung, dropped overboard.

Cornish, of all five men alone lived. I had watched him aim a blow at the boatswain's back, and fired, but missed him. But he too had missed his aim, and the boatswain, slueing round, struck his wrist with the belaying-pin—whack! it sounded like the blow of a hammer on wood—and the knife fell from his hand.

"Mercy! spare my life!" he roared, seeing that I had again covered him, having two more shots left.

The steward, capable, now that things had gone well with us, of performing prodigies of valour, rushed upon him, laid hold of his legs, and pulled him off the bulwark on to the deck.

I thought the fall had broken his back, for he lay groaning and motionless.

"Don't kill him," I cried. "Make his hands fast and leave him for the present. We may want him by-and-by."

The boatswain whipped a rope's end round him and shoved him against the rail,253 and then came running up the poop ladder, wiping the streaming perspiration from his face.

The breeze was freshening, and the boat alongside wobbled and splashed as the ship towed her through the water.

I ran aft and stared into the gloom astern. I could see nothing of the long-boat. I looked again and again, and fetched the night-glass, and by its aid, sure enough, I beheld her, a smudge on the even ground of the gloom, standing away close to the wind, for this much I could tell by the outline of her sail.

"Miss Robertson!" I cried, "we are saved! Yonder is the long-boat leaving us. Our lives are our own!"

"I bless God for His mercy," she answered quietly. But then her pent-up feelings mastered her; she rocked to and fro, grasping the spokes of the wheel, and I254 extended my arms just in time to save her from falling.

"Bo'sun!" I shouted, and he came hurrying to me. "Miss Robertson has fainted! Reach me a flag out of that locker."

He handed me a signal-flag, and I laid the poor girl gently down upon the deck with the flag for a pillow under her head.

"Fetch me some brandy, bo'sun. The steward will give you a wine-glass full."

And with one hand upon the wheel to steady the ship, I knelt by the girl's side, holding her cold fingers, with so much tenderness and love for her in my heart, that I could have wept like a woman to see her lying so pale and still.

The boatswain returned quickly, followed by the steward. I surrendered the wheel to the former, and taking the brandy, succeeded in introducing some into her mouth.255 By dint of this and chafing her hands and moistening her forehead, I restored her to consciousness. I then, with my arm supporting her, helped her into the cuddy; but I did not stay an instant after this, for there was plenty of work to be done on deck; and though we had escaped one peril, yet here we might be running headlong into another, for the ship was under full sail; we had but three men to work her, not counting Cornish, of whose willingness or capacity to work after his rough handling I as yet knew nothing. The glass stood low, and if a gale should spring up and catch us as we were, it was fifty to one if the ship did not go to the bottom.

"Bo'sun," I exclaimed, "what's to be done now?"

"Shorten sail whilst the wind's light, that's sartin," he answered. "But the first job must be to get Cornish out of his256 lashin's and set him on his legs. He must lend us a hand."

"Yes; we'll do that," I replied. "Steward, can you steer?"

"No, sir," responded the steward.

"Oh, damn it!" exclaimed the boatswain. "I'd rather be a guffy than a steward," meaning by guffy a marine.

"Well," cried I, "you must try."

"But I know nothing about it, sir."

"Come here and lay hold of these spokes. Look at that card—no, by Jove! you can't see it."

But the binnacle lamp was trimmed, and in a moment the boatswain had pulled out a lucifer match, dexterously caught the flame in his hollowed hands and fired the mesh.

"Look at that card," I said, as the boatswain shipped the lamp.

"I'm a lookin', sir."

"Do you see that it points south-east?"

257 "Yes, sir."

"If those letters S.E. swing to the left of the lubber's point—that black mark there—pull the spokes to the left until S.E. comes to the mark again. If S.E. goes to the right, shove the spokes to the right. Do you understand?"

"Yes, I think I do, sir."

"Mind your eye, steward. Don't let those letters get away from you, or you'll run the ship into the long-boat, and bring all hands on board again."

And leaving him holding on to the wheel with the fear, and in the attitude of a cockney clinging for his life, the boatswain and I walked to the main-deck.

Cornish lay like a bundle against the rail. When he saw us he cried out—

"Kill me if you like; but for God's sake loosen this rope first! It's keepin' my blood all in one place!"

258 "How do you know we haven't come to drown you?" cried the boatswain in an awful voice. "Don't jaw us about your blood. You won't want none in five minutes."

"Then the Lord have mercy upon my soul!" groaned the poor wretch, and let drop his head which he had lifted out of the scuppers to address us.

"Drownin's too easy for the likes o' you," continued the boatswain. "You want whippin' and picklin', and then quarterin' arterwards."

"We are willing to spare your life," said I, feeling that we had no time to waste, "if you will give us your word to help us to work this ship, and bring her into port if we get no assistance on the road."

"I'll do anything if you'll spare my life," moaned he, "and loose this rope round my middle."

259 "Do you think he's to be trusted, Mr. Royle?" said the boatswain, in a stern voice, playing a part. "There's a bloodthirsty look on his countinunce, and his eyes are full o' murder."

"Only try me!" groaned Cornish, faintly.

"He wur Stevens' chief mate," continued the boatswain; "an' I think it 'ud be wiser to leave him as he is for a few hours whilst we consider the adwisability of trustin' of him."

"Then I shall be cut in halves," moaned Cornish.

"Well," I exclaimed, pretending first to reflect, "we will try you; and if you act honestly by us you shall have no cause to complain. But if you attempt to play false, we will treat you as you deserve; we will shoot you as we shot your mates, and pitch your body overboard. So you'll know what to expect. Bos'un, cast him adrift."

260 He was speedily liberated, and the boatswain hoisted him on to his feet, when finding him very shaky, I fetched a glass of rum from the pantry, which he swallowed.

"Thank you, sir," said he, rubbing his wrist, which the boatswain had struck during the conflict. "I'll be honest and do what I can. You may trust me to work for you. This here mutiny belonged to all hands, and was no one man's, unless it were Stevens'; and I'd rather be here than in the long-boat."

"Bo'sun," said I, cutting the fellow short, "the carpenter made the port quarter-boat useless by knocking some planks out of her. We ought to get the boat alongside in board while the water's smooth—we may want her."

"Right you are, Mr. Royle," said he. "Pay us out a rope's end, will you, and I'll drop her under the davits?"

261 And, active as a cat, he scrambled into the main-chains.

But on a sudden I heard a heavy splash.

"My God!" I cried "he's fallen overboard!" And I was rushing towards the poop when I heard him sing out, "Hallo! here's another!" and this was followed by a second splash.

I got on to the bulwarks and bawled to him, "Where are you? What are you doing? Are you bathing?"

"The deuce a bit," he answered. "It was one o' them blessed mutineers in the main-chains, and here was another in the boat. I pitched 'em into the water. Now then, slacken gently, and belay when I sing out."

In a few moments the boat was under the davits and both falls hooked on. Then up came the boatswain, and the three of us began to hoist, manning first one fall, and 262 then the other, bit by bit, until the boat was up; but she was a heavy load, with her freight of provisions and water—too precious to us to lose—and we panted, I promise you, by the time she was abreast of the poop rail.

"Mr. Bo'sun," said Cornish, suddenly, "beggin' your pardon—I thought you was dead."

"Did you, Jim Cornish?"

"I thought you was drownded, sir."

"Well, I ain't the fust drownded man as has come to life agin."

"All hands, Mr. Bo'sun, thought you was overboard, lyin' drownded. You was overboard?"

"And do you think I'm going to explain?" answered the boatswain, contemptuously.

"It terrified me to see you, sir."

"Well, perhaps I ain't real arter all. 263 How do you know? Seein' ain't believin', so old women say."

"I don't believe in ghosts; but I thought you was one, Mr. Bo'sun, and so did big Johnson when he swore you was one of the three at the port main-braces."

"Well, I ain't ashamed o' bein' a shadder. Better men nor me have been shadders. I knew a ship-chandler as wos a churchwarden and worth a mint o' money, who became a shadder, and kept his wife from marryin' William Soaper, o' the Coopid public-house Love Lane, Shadwell High Street, by standin' at the foot of her bed every night at eight bells. He had a cast in wun eye, Mr. Royle, and that's how his wife knew him."

"Well, I'll say no more—but my hair riz when you turned an' hit me over the arm. I thought you couldn't be substantial like."

"'Cause you didn't get enough o' my 264 belaying-pin," rejoined the boatswain, with a loud laugh. "Wait till you turn dusty agin, mate, and then you'll see wot a real ghost can do."

Just then Miss Robertson emerged from the companion. I ran to her and entreated her to remain below—though for an hour only.

"No, no," she answered, "let me help you. I am much better—I am quite well now. I can steer the ship while you take in some of the sails, for I know there are too many sails set if wind should come."

Then, seeing Cornish, she started and held my arm, whispering, "Who is he? Have they come on board?"

I briefly explained, and then renewed my entreaties that she should remain in her cabin; but she said she would not leave the deck, even if I refused her permission to steer, and pleaded so eloquently, holding265 my arm and raising her sweet eyes to my face, that I reluctantly gave way.

She hastened eagerly to take the steward's place, and I never saw any man resign a responsible position more willingly than he.

I now explained to the boatswain that the glass stood very low, and that we must at once turn to and get in all the sail we could hand.

I asked Cornish if he thought he was able to go aloft, and on his answering in the affirmative, first testing the strength of his wrist by hanging with his whole weight to one of the rattlins on the mizzen rigging, we went to work to clew up the three royals.

I knew that the steward was of no use aloft, and never even asked him if he would venture his hand at it, for I was pretty sure he would lose his head and tumble overboard before he had mounted twenty feet,266 and he was too useful to us to lose right off in that way.

Cornish went up to stow the mizzen-royal, and the boatswain and I went aloft to the main-royal. The breeze was still very gentle and the ship slipping smoothly through the black space of sea; but when we were on the main-royal yard I called the attention of the boatswain to the appearance of the sky in the north-west, for it was lightning faintly in that direction, and the pale illumination sufficed to expose a huge bank of cloud stretching far to the north.

"We shall be able to get the top-gallant sails off her," he said, "and the jibs and staysails. But I don't know how we're going to furl the mainsail, and it'll take us all night to reef the topsails."

"We must work all night," I answered, "and do what we can. Just tell me, whilst I pass this gasket, how you managed in the hold."

267 "Why," he answered, "you know I took a kind o' crow-bar down with me, and I reckoned on splittin' open the head of the fust chap as should drop through the forescuttle. But turnin' it over in my mind, I thought it 'ud be dangerous to kill the feller, as his mates might take it into their heads to wait for him. And so I determined to hide myself when I heerd the cove comin', and stand by to plug up the holes arter he wur gone."

Here he discharged some tobacco-juice from his mouth, and dried his lips on the sail.

"Werry well; I had my knife with me an' a box o' matches, and werry useful they wos. I made a bit of a flare by combing out a strand of yarns and settin' fire to it, and found wot was more pleasin' to my eye than had I come across a five-pun note—I mean a spare broom-stick, which I found268 knockin' about in the coal-hole; and I cut it into pieces and pointed 'em ready to sarve. I knew who ever 'ud come, would use an auger, and know'd the size hole it 'ud cut; and by-and-by, but the Lord knows how long it were afore it happened, I hears some one drop down the forescuttle and strike a match and light a bit o' candle end. I got behind the bulkhead, where there was a plank out, and I see the carpenter wurking away with his auger, blowin' and sweatin' like any respectable hartizan earnin' of honest wages. By-and-by the water comes rushin' in; and then he bores another hole and the water comes through that; and then he bores another hole, arter which he blows out his candle and goes away, scramblin' up on deck. My fingers quivered to give him one for hisself with the end o' my crow-bar over the back of his head.

However, no sooner did he clear out than 1269 struck a match, fits in the bits of broomstick, and stops the leaks as neatly as he made 'em. I thought they'd hear me drivin' of them plugs in, and that was all I was afraid of. But the ship's none the worse for them holes. She's as tight as ever she wos: an' I reckon' if she gets no more water in her than 'll come through them plugs, she won't be in a hurry to sink."

I laughed, and we shook hands heartily.

I often think over that: the immense height we looked down from; the mystical extent of black water mingling with the far-off sky; the faint play of lightning on the horizon; the dark hull of the ship far below, with the dim radiance of the cuddy lamps upon the skylights; the brave, sweet girl steering us, and we two perched on a dizzy eminence, shaking hands!

270

CHAPTER XI.

Cornish had stowed the mizzen-royal by the time we had reached the deck, and when he joined us we clewed up the fore top-gallant sail, so that we might hand that sail when we had done with the royal.

I found this man quite civil and very willing, and in my opinion he spoke honestly when he declared that he had rather be with us than in the long-boat.

The lightning was growing more vivid upon the horizon; that is, when I looked in that direction from the towering height of the fore-royal yard; and it jagged and scored with blue lines the great volume271 and belt of cloud that hung to the sea. The wind had slightly freshened, but still it remained a very gentle breeze, and urged the ship noiselessly through the water.

The stars were few and languishing as you may sometimes have seen them on a summer's night in England when the air is sultry and the night dull and thunderous. All the horizon round was lost in gloom, save where the lightning threw out at swift intervals the black water-line against the gleaming background of cloud.

When we again reached the deck we were rather scant of breath, and I, being unused of late to this kind of exercise, felt the effects of it more than the others.

However, if it was going to blow a gale of wind as the glass threatened, it was very advisable that we should shorten sail now that it was calm; for assuredly three men, even though working for their lives as we272 were, would be utterly useless up aloft when once the weather got bad.

We went into the cuddy and took all three of us a sup of rum to give us life, and I then said, "Shall we turn to and snug away aft since we are here?"

They agreed; so we went on the poop and let go the mizzen top-gallant and topsail halliards, roused out the reef-tackles, and went aloft, where we first stowed the top-gallant sail, and then got down upon the topsail-yard.

It was a hard job tying in all three reefs, passing the earrings and hauling the reef-bands taut along the yard; but we managed to complete the job in about half an hour.

Miss Robertson remained at the wheel all this time, and the steward was useful on deck to let go any ropes which we found fast.

"It pains me," I said to the girl, "to273 see you standing here. I know you are worn out, and I feel to be acting a most unmanly part in allowing you to have your way."

"You cannot do without me. Why do you want to make your crew smaller in number than it is?" she answered, smiling with the light reflected from the compass card upon her face. "Look at the lightning over there! I'm sailor enough to know that our masts would be broken if the wind struck the ship with all this sail upon her. And what is my work—idly standing here—compared to yours—you, who have already done so much, and are still doing the work of many men?"

"You argue too well for my wishes. I want you to agree with me."

"Whom have you to take my place here?"

"Only the steward."

"He cannot steer, Mr. Royle; and I assure you the ship wants watching."

I laughed at this nautical language in her sweet mouth, and said—

"Well, you shall remain here a little while longer."

"One thing," she exclaimed, "I will ask you to do—to look into our cabin and see if papa wants anything."

I ran below and peeped into the cabin. She had already lighted the lamp belonging to it, and so I was able to see that the old gentleman was asleep. I procured some brandy-and-water and biscuit and also a chair, and returned on deck.

"Your father is asleep," said I, "so you may make your mind easy about him. Here are some refreshments—and see, if I put this chair here you can sit and hold the wheel steady with one hand. There is no occasion to remain on your feet. Keep that star yonder—right over the yard-arm," pointing it out to her. "That is as good a guide as the compass for the time being. We need only keep the sails full. I can shape no course as yet, though we shall haul round the moment we have stripped more canvas off her."

I now heard the voices of Cornish and the boatswain right away far out in the darkness ahead, and running forward on to the forecastle, I found them stowing the flying jib.

To save time I let go the outer and inner jib-halliards, and, with the assistance of the steward, hauled these sails down. He and I also clewed up the main top-gallant-sail, took the main tack and sheet to the winch and got them up, rounded up the leechlines and buntlines as well as we could, and then belayed and went forward again. I let go the fore-topsail halliards and took the ends of the reef-tackles to the capstan, and whilst the two others were tackling the outer jib, the steward and I hauled down the main-topmast staysail, and snugged it as best we could in the netting.

These tasks achieved, I got upon the bowsprit, and gave the two men a hand to stow the jibs.

"Now mates," I cried, "let's get upon the fore-topsail yard and see what we can do there."

And up we went, and in three quarters of an hour, with the help of a jigger, we had hauled out the earrings and tied every blessed reef-point in the sail.

But this was the finishing touch to our strength, and Cornish was so exhausted that I had to help him over the top down the fore rigging.

We had indeed accomplished wonders: close-reefed two of the three topsails, stowed the three jibs, the three royals, two top-gallant sails and staysails. Our work was rendered three times harder than it need have been by the darkness; we had to fumble and grope, and, by being scarcely able to see each other, we found it extremely difficult to work in unison; so that, instead of hauling altogether, we hauled at odd times, and rendered our individual strength ineffectual, when, could we have collectively exerted it, we should have achieved our purpose easily.

"I must sit down for a spell, sir," said Cornish. "I can't do no more work yet."

"If we could only get that top-gallant sail off her," I exclaimed, looking longingly up at it. But all the same, I felt that a whole regiment of bayonets astern of me could not have urged me one inch up the shrouds.

278 We dragged our weary limbs aft and squatted ourselves near the wheel, I for one being scarcely able to stand.

"Mr. Royle," said Miss Robertson, "will you and the others go down into the cabin and get some sleep? I will keep watch, and promise faithfully to wake you the moment I think necessary."

"Bo'sun," I exclaimed, "do you hear that? Miss Robertson wants us to turn in. She will keep watch, she says, and call us if a gale comes!"

"God bless her!" said the boatswain. "I called her a wonder just now, and I'll call her a wonder again. So she is! and though she hears me speak, and may think me wantin' in good manners, I'll say this—an' tired as I am I'd fight the man now as he stood who'd contradict me—that she's just one o' the best—mind, Jim, I say the best—o' the werry properest kind o'279 gals as God Almighty ever made, a regular real woman to the eye, and a sailor in her heart. And by the livin' Moses, Jim, if you can tell me now to my face that you would ha' let her sink in this here wessel, I'll chuck you overboard, you willin! so say it!"

"I don't want to say it," muttered Cornish, penitentially. "I never thought o' the lady. I forgot she were on board. Mr. Bo'sun, don't say no more about it, please. I've done my duty I hope, Mr. Royle. I've worked werry hard considerin' my bad wrist. I'd liefer fight for the lady than agin her, now that I see wot she's made of. 'Bygones is bygones,' as the cock as had his eye knocked out in a fight said, when he looked about and couldn't see nothen of it; and if you call me a willin, well and good; I'll not arguey, for I dare say you ain't fur wrong, mate."

280 "Mr. Royle, you have not answered me. Will you and the others lie down and sleep whilst I watch?"

"Not yet, Miss Robertson. By-and-by, perhaps. We have more work before us, and are only resting. Steward!"

He came from behind the companion, where I think he had fallen asleep.

"Yes, Mr. Royle, sir."

"Cut below and mix all hands a jug of brandy-and-water, and bring some biscuits. Here, bo'sun, is some tobacco. Smoke a pipe. Fire away, Cornish. It's more soothing than sleep, mates."

"The lightning's growin' rayther powerful," said the boatswain, looking astern as he loaded his pipe.

"Don't it look as if it wur settin' away to the eastards?" exclaimed Cornish.

"No," I replied, watching the lurid gleams lighting up the piled-up clouds.281 "It's coming after us dead on end, though slowly enough."

I pulled out my watch and held it close to the binnacle.

"Half-past two!" I cried, amazed at the passage of time. "Upon my word, I didn't think it was twelve o'clock yet. Miss Robertson, I know I cannot induce you to go below; but you must allow me to relieve you for a spell at the wheel. I can sit and steer as well as you. You'll find this grating comfortable."

Saying which I pulled out some flags from the locker, made a kind of cushion for her back, and I then took her chair, keeping the wheel steady with my foot.

There was less wind than there had been half an hour before; enough to give the vessel steerage-way, and that was all.

We were heading S.E., the wind, or what there was of it, upon the port-quarter.282 There was every promise of a calm falling again, and this I should not have minded, nor the lightning either, which might well have been the play of a passing thunderstorm, had it not been for the permanent depression of the mercury.

The air was very warm, but less oppressive than it had been; the sea black and even, and the heavens with a stooping, murky aspect.

It was some comfort to me, however, to look aloft, and see the amount of canvas we had taken off the ship. If we could only manage to pull up our strength again, we might still succeed in furling the main top-gallant sail, and reefing the topsail before change of weather came.

The steward made his appearance with the spirits and biscuit; and Miss Robertson went below, whispering to me as she passed, that she wished to look at her283 father, and that she would return in a few minutes.

"Now that the lady's gone, Mr. Royle," exclaimed the boatswain as soon as she had left the deck, "let's talk over our situation, and think what's to be done."

The steward squatted himself on his hams like a coolie, and posed himself in an attitude of eager attention.

"Quite right, bo'sun," I replied. "I have been thinking during the time we have been at work, and will tell you what my plans are. At noon yesterday—that will be fifteen hours ago—the Bermuda Islands bore as true as a hair west-half-south. We hove to with the ship's head to the norrard and westward, and made some way at that, and taking the run we have made to-night, I allow that if we head the ship west by north we shall make the islands, with anything like a breeze, some time on Monday morning."

284 "But, if we're just off the coast of Florida," said Cornish, "why couldn't we turn to and run for the West Indie Islands?"

"Which is nearest, I wonders," exclaimed the boatswain, "the West Hindie Islands or the kingdom of Jericho?"

"It's 'ardly a time for jokin'," remonstrated the steward.

"I don't know that I said anything funny," observed Cornish, warmly.

"Well, then, wot do you mean by talking o' the West Hindie Islands?" cried the boatswain.

"Wot do I mean?" retorted the other; "why, wot I says. Here we are off the coast of Floridy——"

"Off the coast o' your grandmother! Shut up, mate, and let Mr. Royle speak. You know nothen about it."

"The Bermudas are nearer to hand than the West Indies," I continued, not choosing285 to explain. "What we have to do, then, the moment we can use our legs, is to haul the ship round. How is the wind now? N.N.W. Well, she will lie properly. And as soon as ever it comes daybreak, we must run up a signal of distress, and keep it flying. What more can we do?"

"I suppose," said the boatswain, doubtfully, sucking so hard at his pipe that it glowed like a steamer's red light under his nose, "you wouldn't like to wenture on a run to the English Channel, Mr. Royle? It would be airning some kind o' fame, and perhaps a trifle o' money from the owners, if it wur to git about that three hands—well, I'll ax the steward's pardon, and say four—that four hands brought this here blessed ship and her walleyable cargo out o' a rigular knock-down mutiny, all aways up the Atlantic Ocean, into the Henglish Channel, and landed her safe in the West286 Hindie Docks. I never see my name in print in my life——"

"What's your true name, Mr. Bo'sun?" inquired the steward.

"Joshua, or Jo Forward, young feller; sometimes called Forrard, sometimes Jo, and on Sundays Mister."

"I know a Forward as lives at Blackwall," said the steward.

"Do yer? Well, then, now you knows two. Wot I was sayin', Mr. Royle, was, I never see my name in print in my life, and I should like to see it regular wrote down in the newspapers. Lloyd's is always my weekly pennorth ashore."

He knocked the hot ashes into the palm of his hand, scrutinised it earnestly to see that there was no tobacco left in it, and tossed it away.

"A good deal, sir," said the steward, in a thin voice, "is to be said about the lady we287 saved. The saving of her alone, would make 'eros of us in the public mind."

"Wot do you call us—'eros?" exclaimed the boatswain.

"Yes, sir, 'eros!"

"What's the meaning of that word, Mr. Royle?—any relation to earwigs?"

"He means heroes," I replied. "Don't you, steward?"

"I did more than mean it—I said it, sir," exclaimed the steward.

"That's how the Chaneymen talk, and quarrel with you for not followin' of their sense. Wot do you think of my notion, Jim, of sailin' this wessel to England?" said the boatswain.

Cornish made no answer. I saw him, in the pale light diffused around the binnacle, wipe his mouth with the back of his hand, and shift uneasily on his seat. I could scarcely wonder that the boatswain's idea should make him feel uncomfortable.

288 "Your scheme," said I, "would be a capital one providing that every man of us four had six hands and six legs, and the strength of three big Johnsons, that we could do without sleep, and split ourselves into pieces whenever we had occasion to reef topsails. But, as I am only capable of doing one man's work, and require rest like other weakly mortals, I must tell you plainly that I for one should be very sorry to undertake to work this ship to the English Channel, unless you would guarantee that by dawn this morning we should receive a draft of at least six men out of a passing vessel."

"Well, well," said the boatswain, "it was only a thought; and I don't say it is to be done."

"Not to be thought on—much less done," exclaimed Cornish.

"Don't be too sartin, friend," retorted289 the boatswain, turning smartly on him. "'Where there's a will there's a way,' wos a sayin' when I was a lad."

"If it comes on to blow," I put in, "it may take us all we can do to fetch Bermuda. Don't dream of aiming for a further port."

At this moment Miss Robertson returned. I asked her how she had found her father, and she replied, in a low voice, that he was sleeping, but that his breathing was very faint and uncertain, and that he sometimes talked in his sleep.

She could not disguise her anxiety, and I entreated her to go below and watch him and rest herself as well; but she answered that she would not leave the deck until I had finished taking in sail and doing what was necessary.

"You cannot tell me that I am not of use," she added. "I will steer whilst you work, and if you wish to sleep I will watch290 for you. Why should I not do so? I can benefit papa more by helping you to save the ship than by leaving you to work alone while I sit with him. I pray God," she said, in her sweet, low, troubled voice, "that all may go well with us. But I have been so near to death that it scarcely frightens me now. Tell me what to do and I will do it—though for your sake alone, as you would have sacrificed your life for mine. I owe you what I can never repay—and how kind, how gentle, how good you have been to my father and me!"

She spoke in so low a voice that it was impossible for any one to hear her but myself; and so greatly did her words effect me—I, who had now learnt to love her, who could indeed have died a hundredfold over for her dear sake, that I dared not trust myself to speak. Had I spoken I should have said what I was sure she would have disliked to hear from a rough sailor like me: nay, I even turned away from her that I might be silent, recoiling from my own heart's language that seemed but an impertinence, an unfair obtrusion of claims which, even though she admitted them by speaking of my having saved her life, I should have been unmanly to assert.

I quickly recovered myself, and said, forcing a laugh—

"You are as bad a mutineer as the others. But as you will not obey me, I must obey you."

And looking for some moments at the ponderous bank of cloud in the north-west, of which the gathering brightness and intensity of the lightning was illustrating its steady approach, I exclaimed—

"Are we strong enough to turn to, mates?"

"We can douse that top-gallant sail, I dare say," answered the boatswain. "Up on your pins, steward."

And we trooped along to the main-deck.

The spell of rest, and perhaps the grog, not to mention the tobacco, had done us no harm; the three of us went aloft, carrying the jigger with us which we left in the main-top, and furled the top-gallant sail, if not in man-of-war fashion and with a proper harbour bunt, at all events very securely.

But the main-topsail was another matter. All three of us had to lay out to windward to haul taut one earring; then skim along to the other end of the yard to the other earring; and so up and down, and still more reef-points and still more earrings, until my legs and fingers ached.

This job over, we rested ourselves in the main-top, and then got upon the main-yard, and made shift to pass the yard-arm gaskets round the sail and stow it after a fashion, though I had no doubt that the first gale of wind that struck it would blow it clear of its lashings in a minute.

Then on deck again with the main-topsail halliards to the capstan; and the dawn found the ship under three close-reefed topsails, foresail, and fore-topmast staysail, the whole of the other canvas having been reefed and stowed by three worn-out men, one of whom had been pretty nearly knocked up by the fight with the mutineers, the second of whom was fresh from an imprisonment of three days in a close, stifling, and rat-swarming coal-hole, whilst the third had received such a crack on his wrist as would have sent any man but an English sailor to his hammock and kept him ill and groaning for a month.

END OF VOL. II.

Printed in Great Britain
by Amazon